W9-APT-350

GASPARILLA'S GOLD

This book is a work of fiction. Names, characters, businesses, organizations, places, events and incidents are either the product of the author's imagination or, in the case of historical events or persons, used fictitiously. Any resemblance to actual events or persons, living or dead, is likewise intended fictitiously.

The Lexile Framework for Reading® Lexile measure® 500L

For further information, contact:
Tumblehome Learning, Inc.
201 Newbury St, Suite 201
Boston, MA 02116
http://www.tumblehomelearning.com

Library of Congress Control Number: 2016940069

ISBN 978-1-943431-19-9

Markle, Sandra
Gasparilla's Gold / Sandra Markle - 1st ed

Cover Art: Chi-Jung Lee 李其融

Interior Illustrations: Sandra Markle

Printed in Taiwan

10 9 8 7 6 5 4 3 2 1

Dedication

With love, for my husband Skip Jeffery

GASPARILLA'S GOLD

By
Sandra Markle

TUMBLEHOME | e a r n i n g, Inc.

Contents

ONE

An alligator big as a car is waddling onto the road right in front of me. "Hey!" I shout and Aunt Willie yanks the steering wheel hard right. The pickup truck we're riding in skids off the road. Misses the gator. Barely.

"You okay?" My aunt steers back onto the road. She gives me another worried look. About the zillionth one since she's picked me up at the airport.

I nod to make her happy.

So she doesn't feel like she has to talk to me, I slide over close enough to the door to rest my elbow on the open window. I lean my head out. I can see why dogs like it. Even oven-hot, I like the blast of air on my face. I open my mouth to see if I'll catch any bugs. I also squint to see what's beyond the scrubby bushes edging the road. We've just crossed the bridge from the mainland to the island. But there's only a peek of the ocean now in the pickup's side mirror. Most of what I see edging the road are scrubby pines.

And I'm going to spend the whole summer here.

We turn onto a narrow road that's even bumpier than the one we leave behind. But this road's different in another way. It's completely lined with really big trees. They're not pines either, because they're stretching leafy branches out so far they touch above the road. It's like we're in a green tunnel.

My aunt pokes my shoulder so I'll look at her. "Awesome, huh? These live oaks are over a hundred years old. I totally love them, don't you? I mean, think of all the history they've seen, all the storms they've endured."

Yeah, the trees are cool. But not worth getting all gushy about.

Then we're out of the trees and bumping to a stop in front of a two-story white house with a porch sprawling across the entire front.

"This is it." Aunt Willie switches off the engine. "Wahkullah House."

"What's it called? Waw-cool?" I drag my duffel bag off the seat as I climb out.

"Wahkullah. It's Seminole Indian for mystery, which is fitting."

"How come?"

"Supposedly there's a spirit in the house that controls what happens here."

"You're kidding!"

"It's what the locals told me."

I come full stop fast enough to kick up sand. "So the place is haunted."

"No. More like instilled with an intriguing history." Aunt Willie takes my duffel from me and heads for the porch. So I tag along.

"I've never sensed anything in the house but Fiona claims she has. She says she feels it's friendly."

"Who's Fiona?"

"She's a girl from the village who helps me out. She'll be here tomorrow morning and I know you'll like her. She can be a little, well, quirky, but I've decided to find it charming. And she totally loves all the animals." Aunt Willie sets my bag on the bottom porch step. "Come on. Wahkulla House is right on the edge of the island's nature preserve. It'll be dark too quick to go exploring tonight but there's something I can show you."

"Wait!" I follow her down a trail. "We can't just leave my bag out here, can we?"

"Who's going to bother it? Nobody lives within three miles except a sculptor, and he's a good friend." Aunt Willie waves for me to follow. "This way." She shoves through tall bushes and is immediately out of sight.

I stop. Stand where I am. But that makes me alone in this jungle place full of spooky noises. And who knows what else.

So when she calls to me again, I shove through the bushes too.

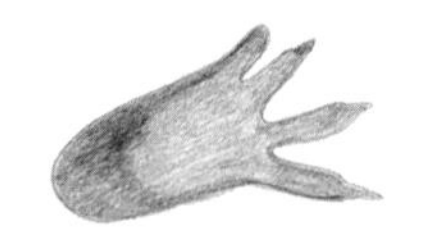

TWO

Two steps and I'm knee deep in ferns and swatting a cloud of bugs. "Aunt Willie?"

"Over here. Across the bridge and into the woods. Be careful you don't trip. There's lots of tree roots poking up."

If I fall and break my leg, can I go home?

That thought tempts me for half a second. Then the truth smacks me. Where would I go?

The Manhattan apartment belongs to somebody else now. Dad's in Seattle, starting his new job and finding us a place to live.

I trot across the wooden bridge over the stream and immediately trip. Spit out a word I'm never supposed to say. I'm pushing off the ground when Aunt Willie grabs me under the arms and hauls me the rest of the way up. I figure I'm about to get yelled at for swearing. But she only brushes me off.

"You okay?"

I bob my head.

"Good. We'll go see Bambi first. I've got some old towels in the Forest Cabin." She waves for me to follow and takes off again.

Bambi?

Forest cabin?

"I'm going back to the house." I set off powered by a full head of pissed-off. Then halfway back wading through the ferns something low-slung, and *big*, crashes past me. I get a shiver at the sight of this tawny, low-to-the-ground animal that is all rippling muscles. Quick as a blink it's gone. Leaving the ferns—and me—quaking.

It takes me a whole minute sucking air before I can even gasp, "What was that?" And then a girl strolls up.

"What was what?" She looks to be about my age. Twelve. But she's, well, filling out in a way that's hard not to notice.

"You didn't see it? It was right there." I point. "And it was really—uh—wild."

Now she looks interested. "Was it a ghost?"

I shake my head. "Some kind of animal."

She smiles and the world brightens. "Caspar must be back. He's a coyote Willie found with his foot caught in a trap and nursed back to health."

"She lets him run loose around here?"

"No, silly. That's his idea." She sweeps her hair into a ponytail.

It's—cross my heart—the color of honey.

She anchors her hair with a band she tugs off her wrist. "His foot's all healed up but no matter how far into The Preserve Willie takes him, dear old Caspar always comes back."

I shake my head. I'm about to tell her I'm pretty sure that wasn't a coyote. But before I can get to that, she sticks out her hand, like she wants to shake. So, of course, I've got to be polite.

"I'm Fiona. You must be Gus." She looks up at me because I'm maybe half-a-head taller.

All I can do is stare because touching her gives me a jolt just like scuffing across a carpet and touching a metal doorknob.

"Hey, I'm trying to be nice." She flips back that amazing hair. "But if you want to be rude and not talk to me, I'm out of here."

"Wait!" My ears heat up when she stops and turns around to face me. "I'm Gus."

There's rustling and footsteps behind me. Then Aunt Willie marches up. "I wondered where you went." Aunt Willie tosses me a ragged towel. Then turns to the girl. "Fiona, you were supposed to go home."

"I did. Dad radioed his fishing boat isn't docking until morning." She laces her fingers behind her head and stretches. It's a move that makes her look very shapely in her tank top and heats my ears up again.

I quickly focus on rubbing my hands clean so she doesn't see me staring. Daniel says you never look straight at a girl's parts. You just sneak peeks.

"Figured I'd sleep on the sofa in the kitchen and do the raccoon kits' midnight bottles for you. Oh, and, Caspar's back. Gus saw him."

I poke the air. "Hey! I didn't say I saw a coyote. It didn't look like any photos of coyotes I've ever seen."

"Then what was it?" Aunt Willie tucks her straggly hair behind her ears.

I shrug.

"I'll bet it was Caspar." Fiona says. "And, by the way, Delilah's flying."

"Finally! I have to see this." Aunt Willie sets off with Fiona chasing after her.

Who's Delilah?

Who cares?

Aunt Willie's got Fiona. She doesn't need me to be out here. In the dark. In this creepy full-of-plants-and-who-knows-what place.

Besides, there's some animal out there. Could be close. Watching me. Ready to pounce. And I think it's a whole lot more dangerous than that Caspar the friendly coyote.

I drop the towel and hustle. "Wait up!"

I follow Aunt Willie and Fiona into a little wood, tin-roofed cabin. It's like darker than night inside. "Hey, will somebody turn on the lights already."

"No." (Fiona's voice.)

"Delilah needs it dark." (Aunt Willie's voice.)

"Who's Delilah?" (Me.)

Aunt Willie clamps a hand on my shoulder and I jump a mile high, at least. "Shhh. Keep your voice down and stand still. You'll scare her when she flies by."

At the sound of stuttering clicks, I jerk to the left. Then right. "Hey! What's in here?"

"Look through these." Aunt Willie pushes binoculars into my hands. "They're for night vision."

I lift them eye-high and look. What I see blows me away. The inside of this cabin is a cave. I mean it totally looks like a cave. Then a small-as-my-fist-thing swoops into view. "I see it. What is it?"

"Delilah's a bat." Fiona elbows me in the ribs. "Let me look."

I hate to give up my ability to see the bat flying around me but I hand over the binoculars. Right after that something brushes my cheek. I squeal and duck.

"Shhh!" Aunt Willie hisses.

Fiona whispers, "You're scared of Delilah?"

I make myself straighten up. "No! I just don't like blood-sucking bats."

"She's not a vampire bat, silly." Fiona fist bumps my shoulder. "Delilah's a Florida bonneted bat. She eats insects."

I'm ready to say *Well okay, why didn't you say so*. But Aunt Willie speaks up.

"Delilah's a pretty rare kind of bat. Somebody from the village found her in their backyard. A cat had caught her and damaged her wing before she was rescued."

Fiona adds, "They brought her here, of course. They knew we'd take care of her and we did. Delilah's wing's all healed now."

Aunt Willie's hand on my back steers me toward the door. "Let's go so she'll settle down. We don't want her overdoing, but I'd say she's flying well enough to leave us soon. Maybe next week."

I walk in the direction Aunt Willie's gentle pushes send me. Outside into the moonlight, Fiona comes alongside. "Wasn't that cabin neat, Gus? Wait 'til you see the others."

"There's more?"

"Thanks to Coop." Aunt Willie leads the way again.

Fiona twists her ponytail around her finger. "He's a sculptor."

"How'd he make that cave so real?"

Aunt Willie's smile stretches ear-to-ear. "He's a genius at turning junk into art. He's transforming the old guest cabins. Wahkullah House was a camp for kids during World War II and through the 50's. However, it was abandoned after that, or it was until I bought the place. When people found out I was a biologist and here studying Florida panthers, they sort of assumed I was interested in all the local animals. Pretty soon they were coming by to drop off anything injured or orphaned."

Aunt Willie shrugs. "I guess they were right because I kept them and took care of them as long as they needed to be here. And Coop came along and decided to make Wahkullah House a proper wildlife shelter."

"Coop used to build movie sets in Hollywood." Fiona holds out a cupped hand. "I heard on the radio there was a chance of rain tonight. It's starting."

Fat raindrops splat my head. Run down the back of my neck. "I've got to get out of here."

Fiona squint-eyes me. "You think you're gonna melt?"

I wrap my arms over my cramping stomach and double over.

Aunt Willie rubs my back "Breathe, Gus. You're okay. Straighten up now so we can start walking to the house."

I make myself straighten up. Suck air through my clenched teeth.

Fiona spreads her arms wide. “What’s wrong? It’s only rain.”

“I *know* it’s just rain.” I try to sound mad but my voice cracks.

It’s raining harder now. That stream could be rising. I fight the memory sneaking into my head. The one where I’m running through the pouring rain following Daniel.

Fiona beams. “See, it’s letting up already, so we can show Gus more of the cabins.”

Aunt Willie looks at me with a tight-pinched face. “Let’s go back to the house and see the rest tomorrow.”

“But Sammy’s is right here.” Fiona covers the ten or twelve feet to the next cabin in a dash. It has a garage door and Fiona’s lifting it by the time Aunt Willie and I get there. The door creaks up and slides back, revealing a space with four corner posts that are real tree trunks. At least they look real. The ceiling’s crisscrossed with branches dripping Spanish moss. And in the center of the cabin there’s a pool. It looks real too. It even has plants floating on the water.

Fiona covers her heart with her hand. “Poor Sammy. He has to live at Wahkullah House forever, so Coop made his cabin extra special.”

I look hard for an animal but all I see are twin dark lumps of something floating on the mirror-flat water. “What is Sammy?”

Then I don’t need an answer because the lumps are eyes rising out of the water. A giant alligator’s eyes.

I’m still shrieking when I take off running for Wahkullah House.

Behind me, Aunt Willie hollers. “The kitchen door is unlocked!”

Arms and legs pumping, I run flat out. Even faster when laser-bright lightning slashes the sky. I cross the bridge in a single leap. Well, maybe two.

When I get to the house, I charge up the steps. Across the porch. Before I can grab the door handle, the door opens. There’s a man as big as the doorway. I take a good look at his face and my jaw drops.

THREE

I stagger backwards.

The giant in the doorway has arms bigger around than both my legs together. But it's his face I can't take my eyes off. When I try to breathe, I gasp.

He grunts. "Yep. That's the reaction I usually get during introductions."

I manage to shut my mouth. Swallow. Can't stop staring, though. The guy has a pink puckered scar fat as an earthworm. It's snaking down the left side of his face from his bald head to the middle of his cheek. And only one of his two eyes is looking at me. The other one is milk white.

Behind me, lightning flashes at almost the same instant thunder booms and the lights inside the house go out. So do the porch lights. It's dark enough the man disappears. Well, almost, 'cause I can still see that one white eye of his.

I suppose this guy is robbing Aunt Willie and I've surprised him. Panic socks me in the gut. I swing around. Make a break for the steps and the yard beyond as rain buckets down. Sounds like a million tacks being dumped on the roof. Looks like a curtain of water.

Like that, I'm back to last summer at camp the night it rained so hard everything went crazy.

My legs buckle. I'm folding up. The monster dude from the doorway catches me before I land. Hauls me inside. Shuts the door.

Next thing I know I'm sitting on a sofa. I'm in my aunt's kitchen. I know that because even in the dark I can see white cupboards, a stove, and a table with chairs around it. The guy sits down next to me and—I swear—the sofa groans like it's going to snap in two.

He holds up a hand big as my baseball mitt. "It's okay, Gus. I brought you inside because Willie told me how it is with you and storms."

It's not storms that scare me. It's what they make me remember.

I look him straight in his eye—his one good one—'cause I'm gonna tell him that. But there's another flash. It's as if that lightning snakes down the scar on his face. I gasp. I don't mean to. Just do.

The guy holds up both big hands now. "It's okay. You'll get used to me in a bit. And the storm will pass pretty quick."

I'm going to ask him how he can be so sure of that but the kitchen door bangs open and I freak. Double up. Hug my knees.

"What's going on? Gus can't be in the dark." It's Aunt Willie's voice.

"No choice. Power's out."

"Phooey! Would have to happen on his first night here."

I want to yell *Stop talking about me,* but the words stick in my throat.

There's banging. And rummaging. I straighten up to see what's going on.

A lightning flash reveals Fiona and Aunt Willie both poking around in kitchen drawers. "Have you found the flashlight yet?" Aunt Willie asks.

Fiona shuts her drawer. "Hey, how about candles?"

"Brilliant, Fiona."

It goes dark again. Thunder rumbles. Then Aunt Willie trots out of the deepest, darkest shadows. "This will make you feel better."

She lines up the three fat, white candles on the coffee table in front of me. Fiona slips a little plate under each one. Hands her matches.

"I've got it." The big guy pulls out a lighter. Lights the candles for her.

"Thanks, Coop."

I squint at him. His damaged eye looks gold in the candlelight. "You're the sculptor?"

"That's me. Say, you're looking better now."

"Everyone looks good in candlelight. I read that." Fiona says.

With a crackle and pop, the light by the sofa comes on. Plus a black iron chandelier hanging over the kitchen table glows. "How about that. Power usually stays out lots longer." Aunt Willie picks up and puffs out the candles—one-by-one.

Fiona beams. "It's a good sign."

"Okay then." Coop stands up and the sofa sighs. "Let's eat. I brought over macaroni and cheese for Gus's Welcome Dinner."

"You cooked?" Aunt Willie presses a hand over her heart. "You spoil me and I'm grateful."

Fiona bounces. "I'm thankful too and I'm starved. I'll set the table. Give me a hand, Gus."

"No." Coop stop signs his hand at me. "You sit right there and take it easy. I'll help Fiona."

Aunt Willie smiles. "Good idea. I'm so sorry that storm had to come along and get you all upset on your first night here, Gus. But we'll take care of you, won't we, guys."

"Sure thing." Coop nods. His smile reveals a gleaming gold eyetooth.

I bristle. Stand up. "I don't need to be taken care of. I'm fine."

Fiona flicks her ponytail over her shoulder. "You sure as heck weren't fine a minute and a half ago."

Aunt Willie gives her an arched eyebrow look and Fiona shrugs. "What?"

My cheeks heat up. "Didn't Dad tell you I'm supposed to be the one helping others? The doctor said it's what's going to make me get better."

"Well, no." Aunt Willie puffs aside the hair tumbling over her eyes. "Your dad asked if you could work at the wildlife shelter over the summer. Of course, I know what you've been through but we Harts aren't good about discussing personal stuff."

She plants her hands on her hips. "I guess we should talk. I've never had kids but with my grad assistants we always start by discussing what they want to get out of working with me. Gus, what is it you want from your summer at Wahkullah House?"

"I don't want this." I fling my arms wide apart. It's a lot bigger gesture than I intended. "Being fussed over like I'm *sick*."

Aunt Willie's eyebrows arch so high they disappear under her bangs. "Okay, and what *do* you want, Gus?"

A shiver slides down my spine. It's been almost a year since Daniel drowned and nobody's ever asked me that until now. I take a deep enough breath to blast it out. "I *want* everything back the way it was."

Fiona glares at Willie. "This isn't about his Dad moving him to Seattle, is it?"

Coop sucks a whistle through his teeth.

Aunt Willie doesn't answer. She's too busy giving me a sorry look.

I bolt out of the kitchen. I'm not sticking around for the *things will get better speech*. I've heard it enough. Out in the hall, I stop.

I want to go to my room but I haven't a clue where my room is. A curving staircase leads up to a landing and along that there's a line of open doors. That reminds me of how the stairs in our apartment went up to the bedrooms. So I hustle upstairs. I'm on the landing when Aunt Willie calls up.

"Your room's the second door to the left of the grandfather clock. But don't worry. The clock won't bother you. It came with the house and keeps time but hasn't bonged once since I've lived here."

When I reach the room that's supposed to be mine, I feel inside for the light switch and flip it on. A crystal chandelier hanging in the middle of the room bursts into sparkle. I go inside fast. Shut the door and lean against it to look around. Then I check out this spot that's going to be mine for the summer.

My duffel bag's on the window seat, which I guess means Coop carried it up. But I can't believe Aunt Willie put me here. This room's all girly. The walls are papered with pink roses. The window curtains are pink too and edged with ruffles. And the bed has a white canopy.

Yuck!

I don't know if I can stand to stay in this room.

Not sure I want to be stuck here. On this island, for the summer. Three whole months.

Not that I've got any other options. Aunt Willie's the only family I've got now besides Dad. It's just been Dad and Daniel and me for as long as I can remember. I was three when Mom was killed by a drunk driver crashing into her car.

But I've got a picture of her with Daniel and me I like to look at.

I rush to the window seat 'cause my duffel's on it, and that's where Mom's picture is. Luckily my duffel's not wet. Coop must have brought it inside before the storm rolled back in.

Unzipping the bag, I dig in. Poke through rolls of socks and underwear. Push through the folded up shirts and pants. At last, I find Mom's picture and I tug it out. Take a good look. But then I lay it on the window seat 'cause I spot the hand-sized, leather notebook in my duffel. Daniel's notebook.

There's a rubber band around it, making it open to the one page I always want to see. On it, there's a pencil sketch of me in my room in our Manhattan apartment. I touch the picture right where it shows the helicopter mobile. It looks so real it feels like touching it should make it move.

And I can see my collection of Percy Jackson and the Olympians books on the shelf above my bed. My Xbox is on the desk. Next to the desk there's the rack of weights I pestered Dad into buying for me so I could work on being as strong as Daniel. And I'm holding the basketball Daniel gave me. Holding it like I'm about to spin it on my fingertip the way he taught me.

I like remembering how proud Daniel was of me once I could keep it spinning on my finger every time. That basketball's boxed up now. On its way to Seattle with all the rest of my stuff.

I miss that basketball.

Miss Daniel more.

A lump clogs my throat. I sit down on the window seat and remember Daniel drawing that picture of me for art class. He sat in the plaid chair in my room with his bare feet on my bed. And, all the while he was sketching, he kept telling me knock-knock jokes—really stupid knock-knock jokes. Making me laugh until my belly ached so he could draw me laughing.

My belly hurts now but I'm not laughing.

And then I hear something outside my window. It isn't thunder. More like a throaty cough.

There it is again.

Leaning close to the window, I cup my hands around my eyes and peek into the night. It's clearing and there's enough moonlight to see tall palms, smaller umbrella-shaped trees, and ground-hugging bushes and ferns.

Is that The Preserve? I remember Aunt Willie promising it would impress me. It does. But I'm not going to tell her.

Right then I catch a glimpse of something slipping through the ferns. Something golden-yellow. I'm certain it's the same creepy thing that cut across my path earlier. And even when I can no longer see it I get the feeling it's still out there. Watching me.

FOUR

When I wake up in the morning, there's sunlight streaming into my bedroom. It's so intense I have to squint. But even then I can't help seeing all the pink and flowery stuff around me.

I crawl out of that girly bed and cross to the window seat. This morning I get a better look outside. But it's only a clearer view of lots of trees and bushes and wild stuff.

This is a real Jurassic Park kind of place. I lean across the window seat to see as far as I can in every direction. I'm checking for something wild and golden-yellow.

That's when I realize I'm still wearing what I had on last night.

I lift one arm. Sniff the pit. No way Fiona is going to want to be around me when I stink.

'Course what do I care what she thinks. She's just a *girl.*

But she's a cute girl.

I shed my green shirt and shrug into a laundry soap-scented blue one. And some clean khaki shorts for good measure. Then I dig back into the duffel for the cell phone. The emergency-only phone.

Before I went to sleep, I had time to think about this spending the summer working at the wildlife shelter thing. I know what the doctor said. That I've got something called PTSD—Post Traumatic something. And how it would help me to focus on helping others. Helping animals would be like super good. That was when Dad came up with the idea of me spending the summer here. Helping Aunt Willie with the wildlife shelter. He thought it was like perfect 'cause we're moving to Seattle. And it also gives him all summer to find us the exactly right apartment.

But I think what I need to help with is finding our new apartment.

Besides, what Dad said isn't true. He said Aunt Willie needs my help. She doesn't. She's got Fiona. And Coop.

I would have called Dad last night and told him I want to go to Seattle. Be with him. But I knew he'd tell me to give being here some time. It's been overnight. Way long enough.

Dad's name and number is the only one on the phone's contact list. I plop down on the window seat. Turn my back to The Preserve. Punch to call. While I listen to the phone ringing, my heart gets to pounding. Then Dad answers. "Hello."

"Dad! I—"

I shut up because Dad's still talking. "This is Brian Hart. I'm away from my desk or on another line. However, your call is important to me, so please leave your number after the beep."

I feel the frown dig into my cheeks until the phone's beep signals it's my turn to start talking. I don't know what to say. I thought this number was just for me to call Dad. It isn't. Then it hits me that if I'm going to leave a message I'd better do it.

"Uh, Dad, this is Gus. I don't want to stay here. At Aunt Willie's. I want to be with you. Okay?"

I'm about to end the call when I decide what I said isn't enough. So I gulp air and add the most important bit. "Please. Dad."

The phone beeps again and a recorded voice says. "If you want to mark this message as urgent, press one."

I do that and hang up.

Bam! Bang! The knock rattles my bedroom door. I stuff the phone in my pocket. Stand up right as Coop charges in.

His big feet swish-slap the wood floor. Geez Mareez! Who walks around without shoes in a place like this? There's got to be snakes and who knows what else.

He hooks his thumbs in the straps of the paint-stained coveralls covering his paint-stained T-shirt. "About time you're up. There's lots to do."

I shrug. "Yeah?"

Coop rolls on. "Willie asked me to come over. She's gone to the university. Something urgent about her research."

"Okay. I can get my own breakfast, if I want some. Which I don't."

Coop's frown adds canyons to his face. "I'm not here to feed you. I'm here to show you what needs doing to feed the guests."

"Guests? You mean the creepy animals?" I cross my arms over my chest. "Fiona can feed them. I'm going to Seattle. Today."

Coop drags a hand down his scarred cheek. "Willie know you're leaving?"

"No. Just talked to my Dad."

Coop gives me a hard stare with his good eye. My cheeks heat up 'cause I think maybe he heard me through the door. And he knows what I said is a lie. Well, it's only half a lie. I did talk to Dad. He just wasn't there listening.

"Okay, but you're here for now." Coop waves me toward the bedroom door. "And Fiona's not here this morning. So you're going to help me feed and clean up."

"No way!" I paste on my mean face.

"Way!" Coop makes a *get going* wave.

I switch to my sad face. "I can't work this morning. I'm feeling really upset. Inside." I add a little whine, which usually melts adults.

Coop snorts. "Move!" He stabs the air in the direction of the door. "You said you didn't want to be treated like you were sick. So march. I need your help."

By the scowl on his face, it's clear I haven't got a choice. I march.

Coop follows me down the stairs. "Besides, Willie said to watch out for you. So I am."

I toss him a look over my shoulder. "Yeah, well, you've only got one eye. So what good are you?"

Coop grunts and stomps past me. At the bottom of the stairs, he shoves open the screen door and stands outside holding it.

I stop at the foot of the stairs. "I'm hungry. If I'm going to work, I've got to eat first."

Coop's eyebrows arch. Then he comes back inside, letting the door bang shut. He goes to the kitchen table and snags the biggest cookie I've ever seen off a plate.

"Here. Have a breakfast cookie." He shoves the cookie into my hands. "Fiona bakes them."

I take a bite. "Ugh! Nasty!" The cookie tastes like chocolate, only bitter, and the chunk in my mouth is dry as dust. I rush to stuff the cookie in the wastebasket under the sink. When I turn around, I see Coop's leaving.

"I said Fiona bakes them. I didn't say they're good." He tosses me a look as he shoves open the screen door. "You see her, though, you tell her you liked her cookies. Got that?"

I nod and follow him outside.

FIVE

We cross the bridge and wade through the steamy heat and the ferns side-by-side. Coop and me. I catch him sneaking me eagle eye glances. Well, half-glances with his one good eye.

"What?"

"Nothing." His eyebrows pull together and he looks away quick. But after a bit I catch him doing it again.

"What?"

"You're just like me. Inside."

"You're crazy!" I give a dirt clump a kick. Look back up at the big dude beside me. "What do you mean?"

Coop taps his scarred cheek. "After this happened, I couldn't stand anybody being nice to me. So I started acting nastier than a shark outta water."

"That's not me."

"If you say so."

"You don't get it."

"Tell me."

I shrug. "It's all the sorry stuff, and everybody trying to make me feel better."

Coop's eyebrows shoot up. "So?"

I kick another dirt clump. "It makes it worse."

He stops. So I do too and our eyes meet. Coop nods. "I get that."

I shake my head. "No you don't. I don't want to feel better. I don't *deserve* to feel better."

He nods again. "I get that too. It's exactly how I felt." He strokes the scar. "Like I should be punished for what happened."

Hmmm. Maybe Coop kind of gets it.

I point at his all-white eye. "How did it happen?"

"I was building life-size model fighter rockets for the movie *Demon Tide*."

Gasp! "You built those?"

"And the demon solar sailors." Coop starts walking again so I take long strides to keep up.

"Oh man! Those were so cool. They had mirrors for sails."

"Those were solar panels."

"Daniel—my brother—drew lots of pictures of those ships after we saw the movie. He's gonna be an artist for movies." My cheeks go hot. "I mean he was going to be one."

Coop nods. "So Daniel was a good artist?"

"Crazy good. But what's building that stuff got to do with your eye?"

"I was stupid." Coop fingers his scar. "I didn't put on my welding helmet that day because it was really hot and—well—I just didn't want to. Then a wire snapped."

I feel my forehead pinch up imagining how bad that must have hurt.

Coop points at me. "Uh-huh. That pretty well sums it up. Plus a heap of miserable. That's why I understand how you feel."

"No!" I get a fresh dose of mad. "You can't. Nobody died on account of what you did."

I take off running because I just have to. I run all the way to the closest cabin. It's got a rusty metal roof with creepy vines dripping off it. But it's somewhere to go. And what I really want right now is a place to hide.

I charge inside. Switch on the light and discover I'm standing on a beach. Well, it's sort of a beach. There are palm trees but they're plastic. And there's water but it's in a bright blue plastic pool that's like a little kid's swimming pool.

Coop comes through the door, puffing mad. "You're wrong. Somebody died on account of what I did. Me." He lifts his chin and looks down at me with his one good eye. "At least the *me* I used to be died that day."

I don't know what to say. I chew my lip.

"C'mon." Coop crunches on across the fake beach. "Help me feed Gabe."

I'm going to ask *Who's Gabe*, but a brown pelican runs out from behind a palm tree. "Phew!" I fan the air. "He stinks like fish."

"You are what you eat. And Willie's vet friend says Gabe's a girl." Coop pulls a plastic bucket out of a hotel-sized fridge, carries it over to me and sets it down. Then he plucks a fish out of the bucket.

"What're you gonna do with that?"

"*You* are going to feed it to her. Here!" Coop slaps the small, silver fish against my chest.

"Yuck!" I resist but he squeezes my fingers over the fish's tail.

"Hold on till I tell you."

"I'm pretty sure I'm allergic to fish."

"You're not going to eat it. Gabe is." The football-sized bird is finally directly under the fish with her mouth open. It's like looking into a pink funnel.

"Now!" As quick as Coop releases my fingers, I let go of the fish. It drops, head first, into the pelican's throat and disappears.

"That's disgusting!"

"Not to Gabe. Feed her another one."

"Never!" I wipe my slimy fingers clean on my shorts.

"Okay. I'll feed the bird. You get the scoop and clean the poop off the sand."

I'm outta here is on the tip of my tongue when the pelican snaps her bill shut. That's when I notice there's something not right about it. Like the top is sort of crooked and has a hole in it.

"What's wrong with her?"

"Somebody shot her." Coop picks up the dark green hose snaking across the sand. "At least feed her until I fill up her pool."

Gabe's beady eyes guilt me into picking up a fish and dropping it into her mouth. "Who'd shoot a pelican?"

"No one knows for certain, but I'll tell you who I figure did it." Before he can, the cabin door bangs open.

Fiona charges in, puffing to catch her breath. "Where's Willie?"

"At the university. Why?"

"*They* came last night."

Coop shuts off the water. "You sure? You aren't just being psychic?"

"For *real*." Fiona makes a pout. "I saw them."

"Who?" The pelican squawks and I feed her another fish.

"The turtles." She tightens the band around her ponytail. "This time every year loggerhead turtles come ashore and lay their eggs on the beach at the edge of The Preserve. But today's the second Tuesday."

Coop's groan is a deep rumble.

"That's bad?"

Fiona gives me a *well-yeah* look. "That's the day each month Pinder's Ranch is allowed to take tourists horse-trekking on the beach."

Fiona clutches her hands together like she praying. "Please, Coop. You have to help me mark the nests."

"Can't." Coop hand mops sweat off his bald head. "Got the rest of the guests to feed. But Gus can help you."

"No way!" Fiona plants her hands on her hips.

I was going to say exactly that, but her beating me to it makes me mad. "Hey?"

"Sorry." Her face grumps up. "But Coop's good at finding the nests and you've never done it."

"I'll come soon as I can," Coop promises.

Fiona scowls at me like something is my fault. Which it most certainly is not. "Okay." She pivots toward the door, arm-waving me to follow. "Let's go."

"Hold on!" I kick up a little of the sand for emphasis. "You haven't asked if I want to help?"

"Oh, for heaven sake. "There's thousands of lives at stake."

"*Thousands?*"

Coop shoves the air with his big hand. "Go with Fiona. She'll fill you in."

So I follow her. More like chase after her. Fiona is fast. But I keep up even when we scale a mountain of a sand dune. Then we follow a path edged with sea oats straight to a beach that's flat as a pancake and beyond it is the ocean.

"Okay." Fiona points. "The stakes are over there."

She leads me to a pile of gray-weathered wood stakes that I'm sure, if I were to lie down, would be at least half as long as me. And there are orange plastic triangles tied on them like they're flags.

"These are for marking the nests."

"Why do we have to mark them?"

"So people will stay away." She carries stakes back to where waves are pushing suds across the sand. "There's a big fine if anyone gets caught disturbing a turtle's nest. But only if they're marked."

"And the nests are in the surf?"

"No, silly. This is where you start looking. See that?" Fiona points to twin divots in the sand. "That's a female loggerhead turtle's tracks. Follow those tracks to a nest, which will be like a sunken spot where the mama dug a hole and laid a hundred or more eggs and packed sand over them. Plant a stake next to that spot. Oh, there's another set of tracks."

With that, Fiona trots off. I follow the tracks she pointed out to me. They stop at a spot that looks as if an elephant sat down on the beach. “I found the nest!” I call out and stab a stake into the sand.

“Great! Now, find another one.”

I see Fiona has already planted three stakes, which is pretty impressive. So I go back to the surf and track down another nest.

Then another.

And another.

I’ve just planted my fourth flag and am feeling pretty proud of myself when I hear a rumble. It’s like distant thunder, which creeps me out. But it’s also totally weird because today is sunny. Barely a cloud in the sky.

“Go away!” Fiona yells and, when I look her way, I see she’s dropped her flags and is flapping her arms like she’s trying to fly.

I’ve planted all my flags. I shade my eyes to see what she’s waving at. It’s six horses with riders. They’re running side-by-side, like they’re racing and they’re charging down the beach. Straight toward Fiona. Me. And the turtle nests.

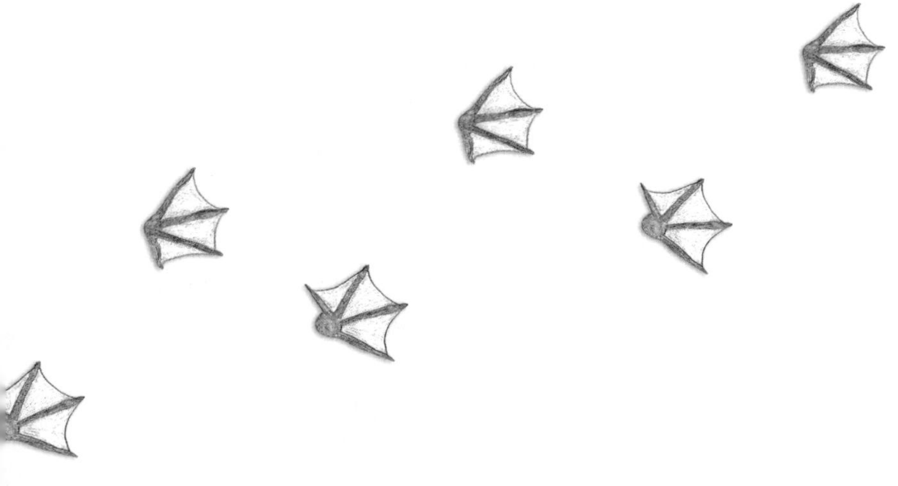

SIX

My heart revs to pounding. I'm perched on the edge of a turtle's nest I was about to get a flag to mark. I look at the sunken, packed-down sand and Fiona's voice echoes in my head. *Thousands of lives are at stake.*

Baby turtles' lives are at stake and I can save them. That is if I plant a flag to mark the nest. Only I don't have a flag. And it's too late to go after one. The horses are almost here.

Then it hits me. I can be a flag. Heck, I've got red hair and I'm stick skinny. I practically am one. And worrying about protecting the baby turtles unfreezes me. I stretch tall and flap my arms.

The horses and riders swerve to miss me. Miss the turtle's nest. They come close, though. Sand tossed up by the horse's hooves stings my bare arms. My cheeks. I stop flapping. Squeeze my eyes shut. But hold my ground.

At last, there's very little sand pelting me. The pounding of hooves on the beach fades. I sneak a peek and see the last of the horses and riders racing away down the beach. My smile pumps up my cheeks.

I did it. I kept the turtle eggs in this nest safe. And knowing I did that makes me feel like happy dancing.

I back away from the nest, gearing up to do the happy dance Daniel taught me. Freeze again when a horse whinnies. I pivot to look.

There's a rider barreling back toward me on a brown and white spotted horse. A ways down the beach, between him and me, a black cowboy hat is lying on the sand. I see he's almost close enough to stop and get off to pick up that hat. But I also see something else. The rider's carrying a flag. *A nest-marking flag!*

That's when I realize the last nest I marked before the horses arrived is missing its flag.

The rider, a boy who looks to be about my age, stops his horse next to that hat and spears the flag he's holding into the beach. I'm guessing because he's bareheaded that the hat is his and he's going to get off to reclaim it. Before he can, Fiona races up. Beats him to it. She snatches the hat off the sand and runs away with it.

Another race is on. Fiona's fast but the spotted horse and rider is gaining on her. He's going to run her down.

I hear Daniel's voice in my head. "Don't be a wuss. Go!"

I run flat out. Charge right in front of that horse. It stops like it ran into a wall. Whinnies. Rears. The rider doesn't fall off. But I can see he's working hard to hang on. Mostly, though, I see the horse's hooves kicking air right above me. My brave evaporates. Whoosh!

I stagger backwards on Jell-O legs. And I get out of the way—though just barely—by the time the horse drops back down on all fours. I feel sick to my stomach. Swallow the bitter taste in my mouth.

"How dare you do that!" Fiona comes alongside me. I'm not sure if she's talking to me or the boy on the horse. Then she steps past me and holds the hat up to the boy. "Here! Take your stupid hat."

The boy frowns down at her. "Keep it. I don't want it with your girl cooties on it."

And with that he kicks his horse's sides and thunders off.

Fiona stamps her foot. "Oh he makes me so mad!"

I stiffen up. Try to act less a wuss than I'm feeling. "Who is he?"

"Dirk, *the Jerk*, Pinder." She punches her hand into the hat to push out the deep dent in it. "And I'm sure that horserace was his idea. He probably told the tourists the flags were race course markers."

She marches back toward me and I wave. "Watch out, there's a nest."

Fiona glances down at the beach. "Right. We need to mark it." Then she looks at me. "You saved that nest. And you saved *me*. You ran right out in front of Dirk the Jerk's horse."

Ohmygosh—it's true. I did. Why did I do that? Because Daniel told me to? Or because I wanted to save Fiona?

Fiona tosses her ponytail off her shoulder as a slow smile pumps up her cheeks. "Did you see the look on Dirk's face when he saw I had his hat?"

"Yeah. Why'd you take it?"

Fiona shrugs. "Because he wanted it and he always gets what he wants. Just like all the Pinders."

"That why they get to bring tourists riding on this beach even during turtle nesting season?"

"Dirk's uncle is a judge and my daddy says that's why the laws are Pinder-friendly on our island. There." She plops the hat on my head. "You need a hat to keep the sun off your New York City skin."

The hat fits well and I like looking out from under its brim. Especially looking at Fiona.

"Come on. Let's get back to marking the nests, starting with the one Dirk unmarked. Once they're all marked, we can help Willie monitor the nests until the babies hatch and head out to sea."

I tag along and chew on how to tell her I'm not staying long enough to see the turtles hatch. I'm thinking of asking if she'd email me. Maybe send me a picture of the baby turtles after they hatch. Then we come to the nest and gasp a duet. This turtle's nest is a mess. The sand's hoof-marked. There are white, round as ping-pong ball eggs everywhere.

Fiona presses both hands to her cheeks. "Oh, Gus. This is awful."

"We've got to save them." I drop to my knees. "I'll dig. You put the eggs in the hole and I'll rebury them."

"It won't work."

I look up. Push the hat back to see her better. "Why not?"

"There's no way to rebuild the nest exactly the way the mama turtle made it. And if the eggs aren't at the right depth they won't be the right temperature. The eggs have to be about 80 to 90 degrees Fahrenheit—no cooler and no hotter--for the babies to develop."

“They’re gonna die?” My jaw drops.

“Hey!” Coop chugs up carrying two plastic buckets. “I saw the horses from the dune. Went back for these.”

Fiona beams. “Great idea, Coop.”

I scramble to my feet. “What good are buckets?”

“They’re for carrying the eggs to the incubator.” Coop points with a head jerk. “It’s at my place. Willie needed me to fix it again.”

“Right.” Fiona tucks straggling hair behind her ears. “You two take care of these eggs. I’ll finish marking the nests. And then I’ve got to get home. Dad’ll be home from the fishing trawler and wondering where I am.” With that she trots off.

Coop hands me a bucket but I push it back. “Can’t you take care of the eggs on your own? I mean, shouldn’t I help Fiona mark the rest of the nests in case the riders come back?”

“Can’t you ever just do what you’re told?” Coop shoves the bucket against my chest.

I bristle. But I don’t say the *Who made you my boss* that I’m thinking. I crouch alongside him. Mimic how he scoops up the turtle eggs and slips them into one of the buckets.

“Go easy. Don’t bust any.”

“I’m trying. How long before the horses come back?”

“Pinders won’t be back with another group until sunset.” Coop plucks one out of my bucket. “Only pick undented eggs.”

"I am. But there's a bunch. We need more buckets."

"Won't do any good. We've already got all the incubator will hold. Let's get them back to my place."

Coop unfolds and starts walking down the beach. I take a minute to check the phone in my pocket. I don't have a missed call or even a text message from Dad. It's still early in Seattle, I guess. I'll call him again when I get to Coop's.

I'm putting the phone back in my pocket when I spot the biggest turtle egg of all poking out of the sand. There's no way I can leave that behind. So I dig it out.

Only what I find isn't a turtle egg.

SEVEN

Coop leaves the beach and heads inland on a skinny trail snaking through tall grass and thorny brush. I follow, hauling my bucket full of turtle eggs and something more.

"Coop! Look what I found!"

When I come alongside him, Coop tosses a glance at the tooth I'm cradling in the crook of one arm. It's nearly as long as a football. It's also so heavy I'm straining to carry it and the bucket of turtle eggs. Coop snags the tooth up in his big hand. Holds it up to examine while he keeps chugging along. "It's a whale's tooth. Pretty old one by how it's gone yellow."

"It's got carvings on it. Words. Numbers too. Could be a message? What do you think?"

"I think I'll take a close look once the eggs are in the incubator."

Coop picks up the pace and I drop back to following him. "How much farther?"

"About twenty feet."

"Really?" I glance around at the jungle that's in every direction.

Coop steps off the trail. Turns around. Before I can ask *What are you doing*, he backs into what appears to be a tightly packed bunch of scrubby bushes. Only it's a gate and it swings out of the way. He holds it open for me to walk through. I do but I don't go far.

"Holy—total—moly!"

Coop's chuckle rumbles and his grin flashes gold. "I'll take that as a compliment."

I do a slow three-sixty. "You are so a genius!"

Straight ahead, there's a line of stepping-stones that are—well, look like—turtle shells partly buried in the sandy ground. But it's the two pretend bugs on either side of the turtle shell path that are something else.

"Wow! I mean WOW!"

Coop head nods to the giant insects that are even taller than he is. "Meet the boys: Paul, John, George, and Ringo."

"I get it. The Beatles are *beetles*." They are so cool. I get up close to one to see all the different kinds of junk it's made of: saws, chains, big gears, hubcaps and stuff. Only their eyes are identical—all red lanterns.

"So do the eyes light up?"

Coop nods. "The Beatles are also wired for sound. When I'm home and want to know if anyone's coming, I switch them on. Then if anyone gets within ten feet they sing *Hey Jude*."

"Crazy! I used to play that on my guitar."

"Used to?"

I feel my ears go hot. Shrug.

Coop gives me one of his questioning looks. The kind adults use when they want you to tell them more. But I don't. Tell more.

I scramble up the porch steps. Wait for him by the door.

His bare feet slap the wood as he follows me. "It's not locked and I've got my hands full. You go on and open up for us. Then, inside, reach up and push the red button on the wall. That shuts off the security cameras."

I do what he said. Hold the door for him before I take a good look around. Coop's house is just one room.

There's a white and silver metal box about the size of a hotel mini-fridge that's right in the middle of the floor. I'm guessing it's the incubator. Coop opens its door and goes to work settling the eggs onto trays full of sand that he slides into the incubator.

He works in silence until the job's done. By then I'm sitting cross-legged on the floor beside the incubator examining the whale's tooth I found. Coop makes a *gimme* motion. "Let's take a good look at that."

Coop takes the tooth I hand him to his workbench. In fact, his house is as much workshop as home. Sure there's a bed, which is all rumpled and slept-in looking. And there's a stove, plus a sink with dishes stacked up beside it. But there's also a workbench running along three of the four walls and a whole lot of tools everywhere, including a big machine-thing hanging from the ceiling with ropes and pulleys.

Coop sits down on a wooden stool beside the section of the workbench that runs under a window. He swings a big, round magnifying glass on a metal arm out from the wall and flicks a switch. That turns on a milky-white donut of light around the magnifying glass and lights up the tooth he sets under it. I lean over his shoulder to look at it too.

"It's pretty badly weathered, but the carvings are still clear. In fact, look at that." Coop touches one spot and his magnified finger looks huge.

"Looks like a tree."

"Uh-huh." Then he points to something else that looks like a couple of towers. "That could be The Sisters, what folks call the identical rock spires that are out in The Preserve not far from Wahkullah House. Geologists think they were probably part of the coastline a long time ago. But I don't suppose that's really what's carved on the tooth."

"Why not?"

Coop turns the tooth over slowly. "Because if some whaler carved this somewhere else and it washed ashore here, he probably wasn't carving a picture of this place, was he?"

"But maybe he did carve it here. Maybe the waves just washed it down the beach and buried it." I plop down on the wood stool next to Coop.

"Maybe. But the tooth's so yellow and weathered that it's undoubtedly really old, so it was carved a long time ago."

"But you can still see words. Like that one." I reach under the magnifying glass and my finger looks huge too.

"I saw that. It's *norte*. Spanish for North. And check that out. If that's the whole word and not part of one that weathered away, it's *oro*."

"Which means gold. I've been learning Spanish in school since first grade. So maybe the tooth's a treasure map. What do you think?"

"Hmmmm." Coop's lips pucker as he studies the tooth some more.

"Look." I point again. "There's the number 31. Or maybe it's 81. Could that be the number of steps to take from one spot to another?"

"I suppose. Maybe."

"And there. That's another word. *Sur*, that's South."

"Could be directions." Coop rolls the tooth over a little bit.

"I'll bet this is a *real* treasure map. There were pirates around here, weren't there?"

"Oh, you bet there were." Coop sits up and focuses his good eye on me. "A man named José Gaspar was a pirate people called Gasparilla. He supposedly buried a whole heap of gold around here somewhere."

"So this could be his treasure map." Excitement makes me bounce. "The map to Gasparilla's gold."

Coop shakes his head. "There's already a map for that. It's on a copper plate, of all things. Anyway, there's sketches of that map in books." He shrugs. "Nobody's been able to figure out what the pictures and symbols on the map mean, though. Plus the treasure was supposedly buried near a place called Lettuce Lake. That's not around here."

"But what if that copper plate was only part of the treasure map." I'm so excited now I pop off my seat. "Maybe you have to have that plus what's on this tooth to find the buried treasure. And maybe it is really buried *here*. On Pine Island."

"That's a whole heap of maybe's."

Right then the cellphone in my pocket buzzes, which has to be Dad calling me. I'd kind of forgotten about Dad. And my message that I want to leave. I wonder if it's too late to tell Dad I've changed my mind. That I don't want to stay all summer but I want to stay a little while. I want to figure out this map. Hunt for Gasparilla's gold.

By the time I stand up and tug my phone out of my pocket there's only a missed call message.

Coop's good eye is studying me when I look up from checking my phone. "Your dad?"

"Yeah. I'll have to call him back later."

"Since you're leaving, I expect he's calling about your travel plans. Probably should call him now."

I roll my lips in tight to my teeth while I place the call. Then Coop turns back to study the tooth some more and I quick press the *end call* button. "Didn't connect."

Coop doesn't look my way. "Poor reception out here most of the time. You best go to Willie's and call your dad."

I paste on a smile. "I'll catch him later. Let's try to figure out the map some more."

Coop turns my way now. His frown tucks into his scar. "You go on. Call your dad. After all, you could be flying out later today."

Heat shoots up my neck to my cheeks. Coop wants me to leave. Doesn't want to treasure hunt with me because he wants the treasure all to himself.

If Coop knew me better, he'd know I won't give up that easy on something I want.

I get up without so much as a *See ya*. March right on out of there. And give the door a shove to make sure it slams behind me. I'm going to go call Dad all right. And I'm gonna tell him I'm not leaving.

No way.

Not until I've had a chance to go after that pirate's treasure. I'm not missing out on that when I'm the one who found the whale's tooth.

I hustle through the gate and am jogging along the path kicking sand when I catch a glimpse of something golden-yellow. It's sitting under bushy, low palm-like plants. Its back is to me and it's in shadows. But I can still see it well enough to know it's a big cat.

Fear slams me. I freeze.

What if it heard me? Cats have super good hearing. I read that when I did a report on lions.

So do I run? Or keep still as a statue?

But what if it smells me? Do big cats have a great sense of smell too?

"Gus!"

At Coop's holler, the big cat turns its head. Its golden eyes meet my stare for a second. Then it slips away into the shadows. Into The Preserve.

I fold up and drop. I'm on my hands and knees when Coop jogs up. "Hey! You okay? What happened?"

I didn't realize I was holding my breath but I was. I suck in air while I point to where the cat vanished. Puff out, "Mountain lion."

Coop hauls me to my feet. "You didn't eat this morning. You lightheaded?"

I stab the air where I'm pointing. "It was right there a minute ago. A golden-yellow cat. Big cat. I've seen pictures. That was a mountain lion."

"If there was a big cat like that around here, it'd be a Florida panther. But there's no way you saw one of those."

I brush the sand off my hands. "Why would I lie? I *saw* a Florida panther."

"More like think you did." Coop cups my cheek with his palm like Dad does to check my temperature when I'm sick.

I pull away. "I swear. There was a Florida panther."

Coop shakes his head. "Willie's research grant is to find and study any of those cats still living on the island. She's been at it two years and nothing. Not even scat. You know—."

"Yeah, I know scat's poop." I brush off my sandy knees. "And I know what I saw."

Coop sucks a clicking sound. "But, sometimes, you just think you see things. Get all scared. Willie said so."

It's not like I hallucinate. Not like that, at all. But I can't push the words out to explain. I shake my head. Clamp my teeth together to stop my chin's quivering.

Coop grips my shoulder. "It's how you coped. I mean gee… what happened to you when you were swept away by that flash flood. And your brother drowning. It must have been really awful for you."

I hear the *sorry* in his voice. Bristle. Spit out, "I saw a Florida panther. For real. I'm gonna go tell Aunt Willie when she gets back. She'll believe me."

Coop holds up both hands like he's surrendering. "Sure. Okay. But come back to my place first. I found something on the tooth I want to show you."

EIGHT

I follow Coop through the door this time. "What'd you find?"

"Sit over there."

"Why?"

"Sit!"

I sit on the stool by the workbench where I sat before. Watch Coop hustle across to his kitchen. He takes a glass out of the sink, rinses it and rubs it clean with two fingers.

"So did you find a clue to the pirate gold?"

"In good time. Patience."

Patience. Phooey. I twist around on my stool while watching Coop pull a round ice cream carton out of the refrigerator's freezer. Scoop vanilla ice cream into the glass.

"What are you making?"

"A magic potion." He twists the top off a brown bottle and pours liquid over the ice cream. It fizzes so loud I can hear it. Finally, he pokes a red and white striped straw into the glass and carries it to me. Squeezes my hands around the cold glass when I just stare at it.

"Drink up. You'll feel better."

"I'm okay."

"Drink!"

I press my lips around the straw and suck. "It's *root beer*. A root beer float?"

Coop scowls. "What'd you expect?" Then his frown curls into a smile. "It's what always makes me feel better. What Ma used to give me when I was the littlest kid on my block and got picked on." He taps his chest. "Look what it did for me. Now, go on. Have some more."

I suck away. Wonder if a root beer float really can change me. But look what it did for Coop, if he really was the littlest kid on his block.

"All right, you go ahead and finish that." His smile widens, flashing his gold tooth. "I'll be sitting right there." He points at the computer on the workbench. "When you're finished, scoot down here next to me and I'll show you what I found."

I slurp big sips as he walks away. I want to finish fast.

I also think about how Dad would go ballistic if he knew what I was eating. Soda *and* ice cream. He'd give me the whole lecture about how bad all the sugar was for me. Thinking that makes me remember how Daniel kept a secret candy stash in his closet. Sometimes, he'd slip me some.

I wonder, did Dad find the candy when he cleared out Daniel's room after the apartment sold? He never said.

Click. Click. Click. Coop's taking pictures of the tooth with a camera. "Can't wait to show you this." He tosses me a glance. "But take your time. No rush."

I suck the last milky globs out of the bottom of the glass in one long slurp. Set the glass down. Lick my lips clean. Move along the workbench to sit next to Coop. "I'm ready."

Right at that moment, I go from feeling pretty good to better yet. That's because Fiona shoves open the door and dashes inside.

"I went by Wahkullah House and Willie wasn't there so I figured everyone was here."

Coop doesn't look up from watching his fingers tap computer keys. "Willie's meeting at the university must be running long."

"I can't wait to tell her the turtles have laid their eggs. And how Gus saved one of the nests." She beams a smile in my direction but it droops when she points at my dirty glass. "Root beer float? Is this about Daniel?"

I feel my jaw drop.

She sits down beside me. "After you went upstairs last night, Willie told me what happened last summer. That your brother drowned. I'm so sorry. "

I nod. Clamp my mouth shut. Hearing Fiona be sorry is the worst thing ever. I'm going to so lose it. Tears are bubbling up. I've got to push them down. Somehow.

Relief washes over me when Coop changes the subject. "So, Fiona, I thought your dad was coming home."

"He is home and sound asleep, because he had to work packing fish all night on the way into port." Fiona divides a suspicious look between us. "What's up? What aren't you telling me?"

Coop taps one more key. "Look at this."

"Is it a mystery? I love mysteries!" Fiona hustles to stand behind him and peek over his shoulder. "What is that?"

"A sort of code, I think." Coop looks at me. "To make a long story short, soon after the Civil War, two Florida cattlemen met an old Spaniard named Juan Gonzalez who claimed to have a map to where the pirate Gasparilla buried a treasure. The men agreed to help him dig it up for a share and went to get a skiff."

Fiona interrupts. "Getting a flat-bottomed boat means they believed they were going out in the Glades."

I shrug. "So? What's all this got to do with the whale's tooth I found?"

Fiona gives me a big-eyed look. "You found a whale's tooth on the beach?"

I nod.

Coop drags a finger over the computer's mouse pad and a jumble of letters and numbers appears on the screen. "So when the men got back to Gonzalez's cabin, he was dead. They searched the cabin and found both a jar full of gold coins and a copper plate engraved with this."

O-X-NXW 1/4 W _UER _UAR
LEGUA 1/10
O-X-SWXW _UER _UAR
HASTA X

I point at the screen. "That's not a treasure map."

"People think it is." Fiona pushes back hair straggling over her face. "It's printed in the newspaper every year before the Gasparilla Pirate Festival in Tampa. Only nobody's ever figured it out to dig up the treasure."

Coop's gold eyetooth sparks. "Maybe, not until now. Could be it's a code for how to use the actual treasure map."

I feel my eyes go big. "You think the carvings on the whale tooth are the pirate guy's map?"

Fiona's face scrunches. "The tooth you found is a map?"

"It's got pictures and words carved on it."

She tosses back her ponytail. "That's way cool!"

"It's definitely interesting. I'll show you." Coop punches more computer keys and three different views of the tooth appear on the screen. They begin to move like ducks bobbing on a pond. Until, all at once, they slide over each other and hook together like pieces in a jigsaw puzzle.

"That's sick!" I lean over Coop's shoulder to point. "The carvings on the tooth are definitely a map. And there's the copper plate's O-X-SWXW."

Coop nods. "When the map pieces went together so did those letters, and in exactly the same order."

Fiona whoops and, with arms stretched high, twirls around. "We're gonna be richer than zillionaires."

Her happy is contagious, so when she grabs me and tugs me into a dance I jig with her.

"Okay, cool it, you two. What we've got isn't enough."

Fiona plants both feet and drops my hands. "What do you mean?"

"There's nothing else from that code on the map." Coop slides his finger across the computer mouse pad until the images of the map and the code are side by side. "And nothing shows where the treasure's buried. You know, "X" marks the spot."

Fiona leans close to the screen. I lean around her to point. "I saw the word *ver* on the copper plate. That's Spanish for *look see*."

Fiona's head bobs. "Gus is right. That must mean something."

Coop taps the screen. "One thing's for sure, if the tooth is the real map, it shows the area around here. Those have to be the rock formations called The Sisters. There's nothing like those anywhere near Lettuce Lake where everyone thinks Gasparilla buried his gold."

"It's like we were meant to find that tooth." I stuff my hands in my pockets to hide that my cell phone is buzzing again.

But Fiona notices anyway. "That your phone?"

"Yeah. My dad checking up on me. Bad reception out here, though." I shrug. "I'll call him from Aunt Willie's." I give Coop a look I hope he understands means *Don't tell her I'm leaving.*

Fiona's eyebrows pinch together as she divides a worried look between Coop and me. "Everything okay?"

I say, "Let's figure out where the treasure is and go dig it up."

Fiona's worried look vanishes. "Let's!"

Coop's fingers drum the workbench. "It's not that easy. Even if we completely decipher the code, there's another problem. Take a look."

Fiona and I lean in again. She groans. "There's like a hole in the map."

Coop nods. "Goes to figure if you make a map and a separate code to decipher it, you want finding the treasure to be hard."

I hold up fingers like I'm pinching air. "But that empty spot is only this tiny part of the map, so how hard can it be?"

Fiona straightens up. "Have you taken a good look at The Preserve?"

"Hard not to. It's all around Aunt Willie's. It's kind of jungly."

"That's an understatement."

Coop adds, "Besides jungle, there's swamp."

"With alligators, water moccasins, rattlesnakes, black widow spiders, bark scorpions." Fiona counts off the list on her fingers. Then she wiggles all ten. "And lots more you do *not* want to meet."

Coop turns on his stool to face us. "You definitely can't just go poking around."

"But imagine if we could figure out the code." Fiona plops down on the stool next to Coop and cups her hands over her knees. "The stories say the treasure is gold and jewels."

Coop says, "It'd be a fortune, all right."

Fiona's smile bursts out again sun bright. "I know what I'd do with my share. I'd buy a charter boat. Then my dad wouldn't have to work on the fishing trawler. He could take people out fishing—day trips only. What would you buy with your share?"

Coop spreads his muscled arms wide. "I'd buy this piece of land from the Pinders. Stop being a squatter and worrying they could kick me off, if it suited them."

I back up. "You're sneaking living here?"

"Oh, they know I'm here. They overlook it because I fix things for them for free. But knowing Pinders there's no guarantees." Coop slaps a hand down on the workbench. "But if I did own this land I'd build a house that would blow you away."

Fiona stops wrapping a lock of her hair around her finger to poke my arm. "What about you?"

"Me?" I back up another step. "Nothing."

Her eyes narrow to squints. "Nothing?"

"He probably wants to think about it," Coop says.

Right then the screen door creaks open and we all look. Aunt Willie is standing there dressed in a go-to-a-business-meeting dark skirt and a white long-sleeved blouse. But Aunt Willie's also barefoot and carrying her high heels. Plus her long hair looks like she was blown in by a tornado.

BANG! Her shoes hit the wood floor and Aunt Willie plants her hands on her hips. "Can somebody fix me a root beer float? I just got terrible news."

NINE

Setting down the half empty root beer glass, Aunt Willie sweeps a look across the table at Coop, Fiona and me. "Guess I'll live."

Fiona teepees her arms and rests her chin on her hands. "Tell us. What happened that was so terrible?"

Aunt Willie sighs. "The university has decided not to continue funding my research."

Coop puffs a whistle.

Fiona rocks back. "They can't do that! Can they? I mean, don't you have another year on your grant?"

"I do, but it's pending annual review. And funding is up to the dean of the biology department." Aunt Willie shakes her head. "I get to keep what's been deposited into my account to date. Which, if I pinch pennies, will let me pay this month's mortgage and feed the shelter's guests. But they want the cameras, computer, and all the other equipment back." She points at the incubator. "Well, except that. They specifically said they wanted to support my efforts to help the loggerhead turtle population. So I get to keep the incubator."

"Because it's a piece of junk," Coop grumbles. "It's only running thanks to all the work I've done on it."

Aunt Willie's face scrunches. "If you want to be paid you're going to have to get in line."

The scar on Coop's face goes bright red. "I've never asked you for money."

Aunt Willie works the straw up and down in her root beer float. "I'm sorry. I didn't mean to snap at you. I know how much you've done to help me out with the wildlife shelter. You too." She reaches across the table to pat Fiona's hand.

"I like helping take care of the animals."

"I know. Me too. And heaven knows they need us." Aunt Willie finger-combs back her messy hair. "But I didn't come to the island and buy Wahkullah House to start a shelter. I wanted to prove there are still wild panthers in The Preserve and push for a reintroduction program to expand the population. Then, somewhere along the line, the shelter became important too." She slaps the tabletop. "And I can't stand the thought of closing it down."

"So you have to keep your grant. Which means you need more time to find the panthers," Fiona says.

Aunt Willie shakes her head. "The dean is right. I haven't observed a single Florida panther in The Preserve. Not even any scat." She looks at me. "That's—"

"Poop," I say. Coop must know it's on the tip of my tongue to tell about the big cat I saw because he gives me a *not now* look.

"Can't you try to find other funding?" Coop asks.

"Went straight from the university to the bank." Aunt Willie pauses for a long drink of root beer. "Thought maybe I could use Wahkullah House as collateral on a loan. Turns out my mortgage is bigger than my equity. That means I owe more on the house than it's worth. So no new loan. I'm going to have to close the shelter."

"No!" The word explodes out of me. "You can't!"

Aunt Willie looks down her long nose at me. "Do you really care what happens to the shelter, Gus? I had a call from your dad while I was driving back here. He says you want to leave. You don't want to spend the summer helping out at the shelter, after all."

Fiona scowls. "Really?"

I feel color blast my cheeks. "I did call Dad. But I want to stay now. Honest. I want to help take care of the animals."

Aunt Willie sighs. "Actually, under the circumstances, Gus, I think it's best if you do leave. You see, I've been offered a teaching position at the university, filling in for a woman going on maternity leave earlier than expected. If I take the job, I'd start right away. In fact, they'd like me to begin next Monday."

Coop slaps a big hand on the table. "It's the answer. You've got to take the job."

Aunt Willie shakes her head. "It's too far to commute except for weekends. But even with the cost of renting an apartment near the campus I'll make enough to keep the shelter going. Except I won't have any way to take care of the animals." She gives Coop a big-eyed stare. "Hint, hint."

"Of course you can count on me," Coop says.

Fiona bounces. "Me too."

I go into begging mode. “Please, Aunt Willie. Let me stay. You can call Dad. Tell him you’ve got to have my help with the shelter.”

Fiona elbow-nudges me. “What we need to do for the shelter is to find that treasure.”

“Treasure?” Aunt Willie’s forehead wrinkles. “What treasure?”

“I found a whale’s tooth with a treasure map on it,” I say. “Well, it’s sort of a map.”

“I’ll get the printout.” Fiona scoots away. “The map has part of the code from the copper plate on it.”

“You mean Gasparilla’s treasure code?”

When Fiona plants the map on the table, I point out The Sisters. “It shows the treasure’s buried in The Preserve. Not where everybody thought it was buried.”

“Well, maybe it is,” Coop says.

Aunt Willie gives me a look that makes my cheeks go hot again. “I guess a treasure hunt would be reason enough to stay the summer.”

I shake my head. “I want to help take care of the animals. Honest.”

Coop reaches around Fiona to pat my shoulder. “Gus was a big help today. Fed Gabe. Volunteered to clean up the pelican’s beach singlehanded so I could get on with feeding the other guests. But then Fiona came along and needed help marking the turtles’ nests. He went right along to help her.”

Fiona stretches an arm up like she wants to be called on. “And Gus kept the Pinder horse trek from riding through one turtle’s nest.”

Coop leans in to point down the table at me. "Didn't you tell me you wanted to take over the raccoon kits' nighttime bottle feeds?"

I know he's trapping me into that job. But I say, "Sure."

Coop rubs his chin. "And it's no problem for me to camp out at the house during the week so Gus isn't there by his lonesome. Sounds like we've got all the bases covered, don't you think?"

"I think I'm outnumbered." Aunt Willie grins. "I'll call the dean. And I'll call my little brother—your dad." She pushes up. Picks up her high heels. "Come on, Gus. Let's go find out if you're leaving or staying for the summer."

TEN

To brianhart@yahoo.com

Subject From Gus

Hey, Dad!

You said to email you once a week. So it's been a week. I know you want to know what I'm doing. Coop made The List. It has times for everything. Breakfast at 7. Lunch at noon. Dinner at 5:30. Bed at 9. I can read for 30 minutes after that. Then lights out.

I'm also helping around here. Honest. That's by The List too. After breakfast, I feed Gabe her fish and clean up her beach. Then I refill her pool. Gabe's a pelican who got buckshot through her bill. She's only one of my guests. That's what we call the animals at the shelter. After Gabe, I feed Pepe. He's a skunk that got hit by a car. His tail is stubby but it's almost healed up. I feed the deer too. There's three whitetail. They've been here since they were babies. Once their spots are all gone they'll be old enough to go live in The Preserve. You should see their guest cabin. Looks like a meadow. It has skylights that open with a remote.

Fiona's here. Got to go. More later.

Love you!

Gus ☺

"Here. Give me that guy." Fiona lifts the raccoon out of the crook of my arm. I'm sitting at the kitchen table typing one-handed while I feed the kit his evening bottle.

Fiona's so close I catch that cinnamon-sugar scent she has. It makes me smile. She notices. "What?"

I can't tell her. Not for real. So I quick make up a reason. "Don't you feel how fat Ranger's getting?"

Fiona gives me a smile back. "So you've named the kits?"

"Coop and I did. Two each. Cause of their masks and spots. His are Ranger and Tonto. Mine are Batman and Robin. Ranger's the fattest."

"No wonder. Look how he's sucking down that bottle."

"Yeah. Even when he's done it's tough to make him let go. Like if he holds on the bottle will fill up again." The kit has his tiny toes wrapped like fingers around the baby bottle.

Coop comes into the kitchen carrying a cell phone. "Willie's on the phone. Got it on speaker. Say hello."

Fiona straightens up. "Hello, Willie!"

"Hi, y'all. I can't get home this weekend." Her sigh puffs from the phone. "This job is way bigger than I anticipated. I have to run a weekend lab. I'm so sorry. Gus? Are you okay?"

I nod. Then realize she's not here to see that. "Yeah. Good. Honest."

Coop says, "We've got everything under control here. So you do what you've got to do there. We'll wait to release Delilah till next weekend."

There's a gasp. "I forgot. No. No. Go ahead. And thank you, Coop. Fiona. Gus. I miss you guys. I'll see you when I see you."

The connection clicks off. Coop's gold tooth gleams when he grins. "So Delilah's ready to be released. You two ready to do it?"

Fiona lifts both her arms straight up. "Yes!"

"Definitely." I close the laptop. "I'll get the flashlights."

"I'll put Ranger back with the other kits." Fiona heads for the cage next to the sofa where the three already fed kits are curled up napping.

Once again, I'm glad we no longer have to go out to the nursery to care for the baby raccoons. Bringing them into the kitchen today was Coop's idea. He said he was done trotting outside at all hours when there was an easier way. So he brought over a tarp to cover the kitchen floor. Then we worked together to haul the big-as-the-kitchen-stove cage inside. Made the kits at home.

"Let's go." Coop takes a flashlight from me, switches it on and leads the way outside. Across the porch. Down the path to the cabins. The sky's quickly changing from bright colors to night.

Fiona prances behind Coop. I carry the other flashlight and bring up the rear. I don't just shine my light straight ahead. I shoot it left and right too. That way I stab the shadows. Keep away anything sneaking close.

Even with the flashlight, I've got scaredy goose bumps, though.

I always do outside at night. It's not that I've seen the big cat again or any other wild animals. But I can hear wild noises out there in The Preserve. And I'm even more afraid of what's being quiet. Thinking about that makes me worry. "You sure Delilah's ready? I mean to be on her own?"

Coop huffs. "Sometimes you just have to pick a time and be ready."

We go into the Cave Cabin. Coop. Fiona. And me. I close the door.

"It's okay. She's not loose." Coop flips on the light. The stalactites and stalagmites don't look quite so real with the light on. Delilah's waiting for us, hanging upside down with her toes wrapped around the bars of a birdcage.

Fiona bends down to peek into the cage. "I'm so going to miss you, Delilah."

I get a fresh wave of nervous flutters in my belly. "Should we feed her first?"

"Nope." Coop hands Fiona his flashlight and picks up the cage. "Better that she's hungry."

Fiona leads the way as we exit the Cave Cabin. I bring up the rear again. Resume my shadow checks to the left and right. After what feels way long enough, I shine my flashlight forward so the light bumps Fiona's back. "Where are we going?"

"The meadow," she says. Then she tosses a look over her shoulder at Coop. "Okay?"

He nods. "That's where I figured you were headed."

I'm gonna ask how far that is because there's only thick jungle that I can see. But just like that we're on the edge of a clearing. Kind of like being ants in a donut hole. Palms, scruffy pines, and straggly bushes are walls around us. The treeless area in the middle is maybe a little bigger than my Manhattan school's fenced-in playground. The three-quarter moon is spotlighting it. Even in the dark I can see how green it is.

"Wow. It really is a meadow." I start to pass Coop for a better look but he sticks out his arm and blocks me.

"Hold up. This is a slough, a swampy spot. The green stuff's floating on water."

"Oh." I stare at it. Wonder how it could be so different than it looks.

Fiona swats the air. "There's lots of insects. Perfect for Delilah to get a fresh start being wild."

Coop divides a look between the two of us. "Who's doing the honors?"

Fiona's cheeks pump up with her smile. "Gus."

"Me?" I stop swatting bugs to stare.

She fist bumps my arm. "Yes. You. Your first night here was her first flight after her wing finished healing."

"Okay." Coop pulls thick leather gloves out of a pocket in his overalls. "Give Fiona your flashlight and put the gloves on."

I do. But I don't want to. I like Delilah but touching her is something else.

"Ready?"

No. But Fiona's looking at me so I can't say that.

"Get close."

I do. Coop opens the cage door. Barely.

"Reach in with one hand. Cup it around her and tug gently.

That's it. She's in your hand now. Bring her out and get ready to put your other hand around her too. There you go. That's good."

I'm holding a bat!

I'm scared I'll squash Delilah. Or that she'll get loose. Fly up and bite my neck. Only she wouldn't do that because she's a Florida bonneted bat and only eats insects.

Does she remember she only eats insects?

"Okay. Get ready. When I count to three, you toss her up in the air. One-two-three."

I swing my arms up. Fling my hands apart. Fiona aims both flashlight beams at the bat. Delilah kind of hangs there in the air for a second with her wings spread out. Then she starts flapping. Lifts off. Fiona keeps the light on her until Delilah flies across the meadow and into the trees.

Coop whoops. "There's another success story for the shelter."

I whoop too. Clap my gloved hands together. I'm bubbling with happy right up until fat raindrops splat my face. Then it's like the sky unzipped and rain buckets down.

A voice in my head screams *flash flood*. I remember charging out of the tent alongside Daniel. Then I think about my guitar. It was Grandpa's. I can't leave it. I go back. Grab it. Hold it tight and take off running again. Only the water's swirling around my legs now. Getting deeper fast. So deep it's tough going. I see Daniel coming back for me and work to reach him. There's a wave of water coming too and there's a big tree floating in it.

"Hey, hold up." Coop's grip anchors me so I have to stop running.

I gulp air. Puff it out with one word. "Flood!"

Fiona trots up carrying the birdcage. “It’s just a little evening shower and it’s easing up already.”

She’s right.

“You okay?” Coop asks.

I blink away the drops clinging to my eyelashes. There isn’t a wave pushing a tree out of the swampy meadow. The water is flat and green-coated, exactly like it was before it started raining.

I nod.

“I like being out in the rain.” Fiona stretches her free hand holding the flashlight high up above her head to spotlight falling raindrops. Then I also see her wet T-shirt clinging to parts I’m not supposed to stare at.

I swallow. Choke. Cough.

Coop whomps my back. “Let’s go home. It’s time for us to work on our treasure hunt.”

Thinking about that, I really am okay. I swipe my face dry with one hand and tag after Coop. Releasing Delilah was cool but our evening brainstorming session about where we might find Gasparilla’s gold is better. It’s my favorite part of every day. It’s even on The List to do it every evening before Fiona goes home. Well, home to stay with her neighbor Mrs. James while her dad is out fishing.

Maybe tonight we’ll figure out the key bit. What’s missing in the middle of the map.

ELEVEN

But a week later we're still working on solving that mystery.

I close the laptop before I've even started my email to Dad as Fiona strolls into the kitchen. "Gus? You want me to feed Pepe?"

"Nope. Doing it now."

"Wait." Coop slides the lasagna he's made onto a refrigerator shelf. "Fiona, it would help if you'd feed Pepe. I need Gus to go with me to my place to rotate the turtle eggs in the incubator and help carry back some of my computer equipment."

"Sure. No problem." She shuts the refrigerator door for him. That makes the papers taped to the door flap. Two fly free and flutter down.

I stoop over to retrieve them. Fiona does too. We bang heads.

"Ow!"

"Oooh!"

We stand up. Each with one hand pressed to our forehead. Each holding one of the papers in the other hand.

Coop takes those from us. “That does it. I think we’ve reached treasure hunt overload.”

There are clues stuck to everything. The front of the cupboard doors, the refrigerator door and a whole lot of the walls are covered with something important. Maps. Photos of The Preserve. Computer printouts of the tooth map and the copper plate code. Plus Coop’s sketches of what could fill in the missing part of the map. Aunt Willie’s named her kitchen TFC--Treasure Finder Central. It was her idea to put everything out where we can look at it every day. Keep the clues fresh in our minds.

Coop sighs. “And I was planning on adding more scans of the whale’s tooth.”

Fiona stamps her foot. “You have to! We’re not quitting till we figure out where to find Gasparilla’s gold.”

“We can’t quit,” I tell him. “We all want to find the treasure. But Aunt Willie super needs us to find it. For the shelter.”

“Speaking of that.” Coop drags a hand down his scarred cheek. “We’re getting a new guest. I had a text earlier. The vet’s bringing over a young boar with a broken leg about dinnertime.”

“So, go!” Fiona shoos him. Then me. “Go turn the turtle eggs and bring back whatever. We’re going to figure out where to dig for the treasure.”

I give her a high five. It’s what Daniel always made me do to seal a promise.

Coop and I get going. We pass the cabins. Climb the dune and march along the beach. We stick close to the surf to stay clear of the turtle’s nests that we fenced off with orange nets. I wonder about all the thousands of baby turtles developing inside their eggs in the sun-warmed sand.

"How long do you think it'll be before the eggs hatch?"

Coop's hand wipes sweat beads off his baldhead. "Takes around sixty days from the time they're laid. Little less, if it stays this hot."

The afternoon sun's blasting down. Sweat sticks my T-shirt to my back between my shoulder blades. The ocean looks inviting.

Guess Coop thinks so too. He's barefoot so he just wades in. Plows along even when a wave slops up knee high on his pant legs.

It's like watching somebody have a drink when you're crazy thirsty. I can't stand it. I'm going to stop. Take off my sneakers. Wade into that foamy water rolling onto the sand.

Before I do Coop tosses me a squinty-eyed look that pushes the ocean and everything else out of my mind. "What?"

Coop clears his throat. "Got to tell you something."

I feel my face scrunch up. "What?"

"The vet didn't just text. He called. There's a problem."

Nervous butterflies go wild in my belly. "What?"

"The folks that brought in the boar said they found it on the side of the road not far from Wahkullah House. Vet said looks like its back leg was broken by something with big claws swiping it. He said he couldn't imagine what on the island could have done that?"

My jaw drops. "The panther!"

Coop shrugs his mountain-sized shoulders. "I knew you'd think that. I have to admit my first thought was the panther caught it and these people came along and scared the cat off its prey. But I'm thinking it's more likely the boar escaped a trap of some sort. Pinders set traps where they've got no business trapping at all."

I bounce. "Coop, come on. I've seen the panther. This is proof."

Coop shrugs again. "If there is a panther on the island, you're the only one who's seen it. Why is that?"

I kick sand. "You don't believe me 'cause Aunt Willie told you Dad caught me talking to Daniel." My face goes sunburnt hot. "Like he was still around."

Coop's arching eyebrows shove wrinkles up his forehead. "Okay. I am taking that into consideration."

I kick more sand. Kick it hard. "Well, it's true. I still talk to Daniel. I miss him. Talking to him helps. Only I don't do it out loud anymore because nobody gets that I know he's not really here. Nobody understands that I'm scared. Scared, if I stop talking to him, I'll start forgetting him. Like I've forgotten Mom."

"But weren't you really young when your mom died in a car crash?"

"I was three. But she's my mom. I should remember her."

"Okay." Coop walks out of the surf and comes alongside me. There's no *sorry* on his face this time. His big hand grips my shoulder. "So, maybe you saw a Florida panther out here on the island. I'd still appreciate it if you wouldn't tell Willie about it."

"Why not?"

We start walking again. "Because it'll get her hopes up. And she's had 'em dashed too many times already thinking she was onto finding panthers on Pine Island. We need proof."

"So lets take a picture. I mean make the cat take a selfie."

"Hey!" Coop grins. "Gus, you've got some real smarts. I can do that. I'll use my security cameras." We leave the beach and head up the trail to Coop's house.

"You're gonna turn security cameras into camera traps?"

"Piece of cake." Coop shoots me another grin. "I've got four cameras with infrared motion-sensing triggers, and they transmit images to my computer. All I've got to do is give them battery power packs. Then you can help me decide where to plant them around Wahkullah House."

"Cool." I like the idea of Coop and me being nature spies. "Are we going to tell Fiona?"

"No!" Coop thunders.

"Hey. Okay." I bristle. Then I realize he's not talking to me.

Straight ahead, I see the door to Coop's house is wide open. He stomps up the steps across the porch. Calls out, "Wait here!" Then rolls on inside.

I wait at the bottom of the porch steps. One second. Two. Enough. I power into the house after Coop. He's crouched down checking the eggs in the incubator. He straightens up. "The incubator door was open. Don't know how long. Eggs are still warm, though, so I guess everything's okay."

I look around. Nothing else is okay. "Geez!"

The refrigerator door is open. The bed is on its side. The table and chairs are overturned too. There's stuff from the workbench scattered everywhere.

"You've been robbed."

"No. My computer's still here."

He's right. The computer is the one thing that is still on the workbench. In fact, the computer screen is displaying a slide show of images of famous landmarks, like the Eiffel Tower and Big Ben.

"Geez, Coop. Who'd do this?"

"Well, I'll know in a minute." He steps over a pile of books and rights a stool to sit down at his computer. "Security cameras will show me."

"Where are the cameras?" I look around. Don't see any.

"I built movie sets, remember." Coop points out a lantern, two knots on ceiling beams and a mirror on the wall.

Coop's pecking at the keys by the time I find my way across the maze of debris. He pushes one more key. "Here goes."

Images of the inside of Coop's house replace the slide show. There are only glimpses of three people coming inside. All three are wearing hoodies and Halloween monster masks. There are pictures of them digging through drawers, turning over the bed and scooping stuff off the workbench.

Coop taps the computer screen. "This wasn't a prank. Those three were searching for something. But what've I got anybody'd want?"

"Wait! Go back." I lean over Coop's shoulder. One of the three pulled up his mask for a better look inside the incubator. The shiny inside surface of the incubator's door caught his reflection. I point at it. "I know him."

TWELVE

Back at Wahkullah House, I plunk my empty root beer float glass down on the kitchen table. Lick my sudsy lips clean. "So one of the guys was Dirk Pinder."

"Beats me who the other two were." Coop shakes his head. "More kids, I suppose. Couldn't get a clear take on how tall they were from the photos."

The last of the twilight's glow streaming through the windows is fading fast so Fiona gets up to switch on the kitchen lights. "You said you thought they were searching for something."

Coop lifts his hands palms up. "I said that because they didn't take anything. Maybe it's George Pinder's way of evicting me. The house used to be one of the ranch's cowboy cabins. But it was a falling-down wreck before I moved in and fixed it up. Still, if Pinder wants me off his land so bad, all he has to do is say so."

I trace the shape of the whale's tooth in the water droplets coating my glass. "I bet Dirk Pinder saw me pick up the whale's tooth on the beach."

"So what?" Fiona asks between slurps of her float. "Why would Dirk the Jerk care? He doesn't know about the treasure map."

"Hmmmm." Coop adds more root beer to his glass. "What if he does?"

I lean in close. "How could he?"

"His Uncle Marcus." Coop sets the bottle down hard. "He's Pine Island's resident historian."

Fiona's eyes pop to saucer-sized. "Whoa! You think he knows Gasparilla carved part of his treasure map on a whale's tooth? And that the treasure's buried someplace around here? Maybe he's been looking for that tooth for years."

Coop whistles through his teeth. "If the Pinders thought there was treasure on this island, I guarantee there's nothing they wouldn't do to get it."

I pat the tooth lying in the center of the table. "Good thing you hid it outside in Ringo's mouth."

Coop grins. "Guess I must have had a premonition or something."

Fiona tosses her ponytail with her headshake. "More likely it was the Wahkullah House Spirit sending you a message."

Coop winks his good eye at me. "If you say so."

I tug the tooth close enough to pick up. Which I do. And I peek through the hole in the tooth. "Maybe we're supposed to look through the hole at something. Like the copper plate code."

"I'll get the printout." Fiona dashes to the wall where it's taped and brings it back.

I peek through the hole at it. "Looks just the same."

Fiona chews her lip for a second. "I know. I bet we're supposed to shine a light through the hole in the tooth."

Excited butterflies nearly lift me off my chair. "Yeah. Maybe."

"Worth a try." Coop gets a flashlight.

I stand up. Hold up the tooth. Coop switches on the flashlight and holds the lit end against the hole. All that appears on the copper plate code is a bright spot.

Fiona and I duet a groan.

A horn tooting outside cuts us off. "That'll be the vet." Coop hands Fiona the flashlight. "I'll go get the boar settled."

He hustles off.

"Got to be something else to try," I tell her. "The hole in the tooth is a clue. I feel it."

And right then—cross my heart—the front door that we heard Coop shut bangs open. We charge out on the porch as Coop and another guy walk away from a van, hauling a big travel cage between them.

Fiona and I exchange looks. "That was creepy!"

Fiona holds the flashlight beam under her chin so it casts spooky shadows on her face. "*That* was a message from the Wahkullah House Spirit."

"Telling us what?"

"That our clue is out there." Fiona aims the flashlight beam into the night.

"Where? There's a whole lot of *out there*."

"Oooh!" Fiona bounces. "The Sisters. I just thought of it. Bet the Spirit made me think of it."

I tuck the whale's tooth into a football carry. "Okay. So tomorrow we'll get Coop to take us to The Sisters."

"No, silly." Fiona aims the flashlight at my face and I squint in the bright light. "The Spirit told *us*. That means you and I are supposed to go. And we got the message *now*, which means we're supposed to go this minute."

"No way!" I say but Fiona trots down the porch steps. So I follow.

THIRTEEN

Five steps into the bushes and ferns I plant my feet and make my stand. "It's too dark. We can't go out into The Preserve."

Fiona turns around and goes toe-to-toe with me. "You're scared?"

"Yeah. Why aren't you?" I use my mean voice although it's hard to do because she's so close. And smells like cinnamon and sugar.

"Look. It's okay to go in The Preserve at night if you know your way around."

"Well." I feel my swallow ripple all the way down my throat.

She tosses her ponytail over her shoulder. "I know this place as well as my own house. Dad's taken me into The Preserve at night lots of times. Been doing it since I was little."

"Really?"

"Stay close to me and you'll be fine."

"Well."

Fiona sets off and, though I really don't want to, I follow her. Stick close as her shadow.

There's a path—sort of. We follow it between ferns and bushes. Along a stream. Something slithers making ripples that spoil the moon's reflection on the water.

"Hey." I point and she looks.

Fiona puffs back hair tumbling over one eye. "Probably just a water moccasin."

"Just? That's a poisonous snake!"

She shrugs. "Dad says critters won't bother you if you don't bother them."

Fiona lopes off and I follow again. But I keep checking the ground in case that water moccasin has cousins.

I don't know how long we walk. After a while I figure it's been long enough. "Aren't we there yet?"

"Soon. It's worth it. Trust me."

I open my mouth to say something smart but a bug flies in and I have to spit it out. Then I've got to duck under a bunch of vines. I mean really low vines with sticky webs stitching them together, which means there's spiders. "This sucks."

"You don't like nature?"

"I like it better in books." When I straighten up, she's standing there looking at me with a big grin. Like something's funny. Or maybe something about me is funny. "What?"

"Look." Fiona grabs me and turns me ninety degrees. "There!"

"Geez!" But that's not hardly a big enough word to describe what I'm seeing.

"I told you, didn't I? And seeing it for real is better than any picture in a book."

"Way—totally—better."

Side by side we share looking at two rock spires as tall as—well—Coop, I guess. And they're so creamy-white they glow in the moonlight. Plus they're so close it's like they could hold hands. If they had hands.

Fiona does a sort of point the way ladies show off prizes on TV game shows. "Meet The Sisters."

I stroll over because I have to touch one. I finger trace initials carved into the stone. "They're all bumps and bits like they're made up of a zillion seashells. Guess that's what makes them easy to carve."

"Yeah, that's coquina and they are bits of seashells."

I trace a number now. "Wonder how that kind of rock got made."

Fiona steps up alongside me and touches the rock too. "Dad says it happened because, once upon a time, our island was underwater. When sea animals like mollusks and trilobites and such died, their shells piled up. Broke up. And packed together until they all stuck tight."

"Cool!"

"Definitely. First time Dad brought me here there was a full moon. The three-quarter one tonight's good for seeing The Sisters too."

I moonwalk backwards and Fiona giggles, which is a sound that makes happiness bubble all the way through me. But then I go back to looking at The Sisters. Only this time not just because they're amazing. I'm seeing something else. It's like the stone spires are shimmering in the dark. Then I lift the whale's tooth. Peek through the hole at the rock spires. That's when I see it.

"Oh!"

"Do you see something, Gus?"

I move the tooth and stare at a fresh part of the spire. "O! M! G!"

Fiona pokes me. "Gus?"

I lower the tooth to look at her. "I just spotted SW carved on one Sister. Straight across on the second Sister is XW. That's part of the copper plate code, isn't it?"

"Wow!" Fiona's eyes go huge. Then she squints and whispers, "Shhh!"

I look where she points and see a light peeking between leaves. Somebody's out there in the dark. And coming this way.

FOURTEEN

Fiona switches off the flashlight. We stand in The Sisters' shadows. Stay rock still. I hope whoever is out there will go away.

"Hey, this way," somebody calls.

The flashlight beam streaks straight toward us. Fiona and I exchange *holy crap* looks. We slip through the shadows into the bushes. I'm still pushing on when she crouches down. I go back and nudge her shoulder. She shakes her head. Looks up at me. Mouths, "Pinders."

I don't question how Fiona knows. Only hug the whale's tooth tight and give her a double *let's go* nudge. Fiona ignores me. Teases apart the bush's branches in front of her to peek through.

A throaty voice grumbles, "I don't get why we've got to do this at night. Gonna fall and break our necks walking around out here in the dark."

"Because it's the best time. And it's the only time we can be sure somebody won't come along and see what we're doing."

Somebody is already here. Fiona and me. And if we don't leave we're going to see whatever the Pinders don't want us to see.

I give Fiona's shoulder another nudge. Harder this time.

She waves me to get down next to her.

No way. I look around for my best exit. Pick what I'm sure is the direction back to Wahkullah House. Push into the bushes. Right away I come to a trail. It's a sign. This is the right way and I'm supposed to take it.

I march along. Toss glances over my shoulder. Keep hoping I'll see Fiona chasing after me. But I don't.

Guilt nags me.

Truth be told, Daniel nags me. I hear my brother's voice in my head. *You left Fiona. What were you thinking?*

"That we needed to get out of there."

Man up. (Daniel again.)

"You don't know Fiona. She does what she wants to."

Go back.

I stop.

You know you have to.

"Okay. Okay." I turn around. Start backtracking.

Hurry up!

Daniel's right. Fiona could be in trouble. I take off running.

I never should have left her. I've got to get back. Fast.

FLOP!

I trip on a tree root. Drop the whale's tooth on my way to the ground. While I'm landing hard, it bounces away from me. Slips under a bush.

I stretch out on my belly on the soft, moist ground and dig under the bush. Pray I find the tooth. Pray I don't find any snakes. Scorpions. Or spiders.

Relief floods through me when my fingers touch the tooth. I tug it out. Scramble back to my feet. That's when I hear a strange sound. Kind of a whiney chirp.

I look this way and that. What's out there?

I hear it again and I think I know. It's the panther. Next second, I think, *It can't be.*

This animal has a really wimpy voice. I mean, I don't know if Florida panthers roar. But the big cat I've seen a couple times looked like it would sound fierce.

I hear that whiney chirp again.

Geez, whatever it is sounds more scared than I am.

I hug the whale's tooth. Squint to look around in the dark. That's when I spot the wire cage at the base of a palm tree. It's about the size of one of the boxes I packed my stuff in moving out of our Manhattan apartment. Something's inside. It's wiggling. I shuffle-step a little closer. Get ready to run in case it can get out.

I see the cage door is closed. Whatever is inside is about the size of the Labrador puppy our neighbor got last Christmas. But it's not puppy-shaped. And that noise it keeps making is definitely not a dog noise.

I shuffle closer.

The thing in the cage goes quiet. Squeezes back as far as it can. That's when I see there's something else in the cage—a glob of meat with a wire attached to it.

This cage is a trap. For real. I bend down for a better look.

A little cat face with blue eyes above a white muzzle looks back at me. It's a panther cub.

Yes! Right here in front of me is Aunt Willie's proof there are Florida panthers on Pine Island. If I take it back to Wahkullah House, I'll be a hero.

I flash to imagining Aunt Willie cheering and hugging me. I add Dad being there too. Looking proud.

But I've got to get the cub back to Wahkullah House. The cage is chained to the palm and locked with a padlock. That means I've got to take the cub out of the cage and carry it. It looks scared enough to let me do that.

I hope it is 'cause I'm feeling pretty scared too.

I set the tooth on the ground next to the cage. Get down on my knees and go to work figuring out how to open the cage door. Oh yeah. I see.

I'm about to pull up the cage door when I meet the cub's stare. "Hey. Don't look at me like that. Like you're gonna bite me? I'm saving you from the Pinders."

The cub opens its mouth but this time what I hear is a deep, rumbling growl. That's a big cat sound. Quick as a blink, I'm on my feet. Staring at a golden-yellow panther slinking out of the bushes.

Mama!

That big cat stops. Looks at me too. And she lays her black-tipped ears flat as she studies me with big golden eyes.

I don't move a muscle. Don't breathe. Don't blink. But my mind's screaming, *What do I do? Stay still? Run?*

The panther keeps watching me. Like she's waiting for me to make a move. Then her ears lift—one turns—like she hears something.

Now I hear it too. Rustling. Like somebody's shoving through bushes. Fiona! I've got to warn her.

But what if it's Pinders?

I suck in a breath. Try to decide what to do.

Mama cat rumbles. The cub in the cage whines.

Somehow, now I'm sure it's Pinders that are coming. And they're going to find the cub trapped.

And, right like that, I bend over. Open the cage door. Only I don't reach inside for the cub.

Mama chuffs.

The cub rockets out of the cage. Follows Mama cat into the thick bushes.

The cats vanish—honest truth—exactly as Dirk Pinder and two men carrying rifles arrive. Dirk's flashlight beam smacks me in the face. Even nearly blinded I can see his scrunched up frown. "You!"

"Who are you?" one of the two men asks me.

I swallow hard, getting ready to answer.

Fiona charges up beside me. Points at Dirk and the two men. "You aren't allowed to hunt in The Preserve."

One of the two men pokes the open cage door with his rifle. "You turn something loose, boy?"

I shake my head. Hope, hope, hope he doesn't spot the whale's tooth in the shadow next to the cage.

Dirk says, "Bet he did, Daddy. Bet we caught a gray fox like you wanted for the tourist zoo and he turned it loose."

I stiffen. "Can't be legal to trap in The Preserve."

Fiona comes alongside me. "It isn't. This is a state park."

"Florida might claim it but all of Pine Island is Pinder land."

Dirk grins, "You tell 'em, Uncle Marcus."

Whoa. Is this Marcus Pinder? The one Coop said was the island's historian?

Dirk's dad adds, "That means everything around here, even pirate treasure, belongs to us."

Fiona and I exchange *does he know* looks.

Marcus Pinder grins. "That's right. This island was given to our great-great-grandfather in 1821 for his service during the First Seminole War. Andrew Jackson signed the deed himself while he was military governor of Florida."

Dirk sneers. "That means you're trespassing."

His daddy divides a look between Fiona and me. "So go on. You kids go home. And be quick about it."

Fiona and I exchange *let's do it* glances and hustle out of there.

Behind us, I hear the three Pinders laughing. The sound gives me goose bumps but I stretch my arm out to snag Fiona's arm. When she stops, I point. "The tooth. It's back there. I left it by the cage."

She nods. We go back. But we sneak. Go slow. Stay as quiet as shadows. When we're close, we get down on our hands and knees.

Belly crawl to where we can peek between leafy branches at the cage trap.

The Pinders are gone.

We get up and hustle to the cage.

But the tooth is gone too.

FIFTEEN

When we get back to Wahkullah House, Coop is waiting for us on the porch. He leaps to his feet. Runs down the steps and crushes both of us in a hug before we can get a word out. "I was debating between calling the sheriff and going to search for you myself. I'd just decided to do both. Where were you?"

Fiona puffs out, "The Preserve, and it was my idea."

I pipe up. "But I wanted to go. We saw The Sisters. In the moonlight. Super cool!"

Fiona and I exchange glances that mean we're not telling about the missing tooth. Or the Pinders. Not tonight.

Coop pushes us an arm's length away. Gives us a look that's all hard angles. "Well, you two scared me to death!"

We duet, "Sorry."

Coop gives us a *never ever go off without telling me again* speech. We promise. I'm sent straight to bed while he drives Fiona to the village.

The next morning, Coop's done burning but still fuming. "You do know going out in The Preserve at night was dangerous. And stupid. Right?"

"Yes sir." I pour cornflakes and milk in a bowl. Sink into my seat at the kitchen table.

"Well," Coop huffs. "It's going to take a while for me to trust you again. Either of you."

"Yes sir."

"All right." Coop drums his fingers on the table. "So I'm not going to call Willie. I don't see any reason to upset her while she's away at the university."

I nod while I chew. I'm grateful because Aunt Willie would for sure tell my dad. I definitely don't want him to know I did something I wasn't supposed to.

Coop drums some more. "You email your dad this week?"

I shake my head.

"That's two weeks you've missed. C'mon, Gus. He said for you to email him every week. He misses you."

"No!" I spit out with bits of cornflakes. "He misses Daniel." My ears heat up. "Blames me 'cause he's dead."

"No way."

"Way! It's my fault Daniel drowned."

"Impossible." Coop's frown carves canyons in his forehead.

Milk splashes as my spoon lands in the cereal bowl. "I went back to our tent for my guitar when Daniel said not to. Swoosh. I got swept away. But Daniel got to me. Shoved me up onto the bank. Then a giant tree branch hit him. Pushed him under."

It's quiet for a minute except for the raccoon kits chittering in their cage. Coop's good eye is looking at me real hard. His voice sounds choked up when he says, "Well, I'm grateful Daniel saved you."

"Dad's not." My cheeks go even hotter than my ears. I push away from the table. Bolt for the door.

I'm shoving the screen door open when Aunt Willie marches up the steps and across the porch. The tails of her long-sleeved shirt flap as she passes me on her way through the door I'm holding open. "Thanks, Gus."

Fiona runs up the steps and through the door after her. "Hey, Willie. I didn't know you were coming home today."

Coop stands up. "What's wrong?"

"Something wrong?" I step back into the kitchen and the closing screen door slaps my backside.

Aunt Willie packs us all into one look. "I got a call about Caspar this morning from George Pinder."

"Caspar?" Fiona presses crossed hands over her heart.

Coop sucks a whistle through his teeth. "If George Pinder called, it can't be good."

Aunt Willie plants both hands on her hips "He said his men saw Caspar tearing into the carcass of one of his prize calves. Actually, he said it was a coyote with a radio collar so he knew it was one of my *pets*. If I don't pay for the calf, he's going to hunt down Caspar."

Fiona fans the air. "Poor Caspar."

Aunt Willie tucks straggling hair behind her ears. "I've got to go over to the Pinder ranch and talk to George."

Coop runs a finger around his T-shirt collar. “Give me a minute to put on a clean shirt. I’ll go with you.”

“Thanks, but I’ll take Gus. There’s some family business we need to discuss. We can do that on the way.” Aunt Willie head nods to me. “Let’s go.”

“Wait.” Coop stop signs his hand. “I’ve got a little money saved, if you need it. How much does Pinder want for the calf?”

“I don’t know yet. And thanks. I might need to take you up on a loan.” Aunt Willie heads out the door, motioning again for me to follow. As soon as we’re underway in the truck she says, “It’s getting hot. Roll your window down and listen up.”

I roll down my window but I figure it’ll be easier if I speak up first. So I do. “Look, I’m sorry I haven’t emailed Dad for two weeks. I’ll do it today.”

“That isn’t what we need to talk about.” Aunt Willie tosses me a glance that’s all pinches and puckers. “I’m probably poking my nose in where I shouldn’t. Only I think it’ll be easier on both you and your dad, if you’re prepared for what he’s flying here to tell you.”

I stiffen up. “He’s coming here? Why?”

She tosses me another look. “Your dad’s enrolled you in a boarding school in Seattle.”

I sink back in the seat. Feel like an elephant just sat down on my lap.

Aunt Willie rolls on. “He told me he was originally planning to send you there in the fall because they have counselors especially to help troubled—well—to help you deal with what you’re going through. Turns out they've got an opening in the summer session that starts in July. So he's coming here to take you back with him."

"I won't go!"

Aunt Willie tosses me a peek from beneath her frizzy bangs. "Your dad thinks it's the best thing for you, Gus."

"Best thing for *him,*" I say. "If he doesn't want me around, he should let me stay here. Go to school here too. You need me."

She nods. "I do, but most of all I want what's best for you. So does your dad because he loves you."

I scoot closer to face her. "He *loved* Daniel. Everybody loved Daniel." I hold up my fingers as I count the reasons. "He gets great grades. He's funny. He's super at sports. I'm lousy at everything except music."

Aunt Willie pastes on a smile. "Your grandpa was so happy to finally have someone in the family get his gift for music. He told me how quick you took to the guitar. How good you are at playing and writing songs. That's why he left his guitar to you in his will."

"Wish I never learned to play." I look out the truck's side window quick so she won't see me blinking back tears.

"I want to talk to you more about this," Aunt Willie says. "And we are going to talk more about this. But it's going to have to be later. Right now I'm going to have to deal with the Pinders."

We're slowing down and I look straight ahead. See we're coming up to a house and barn with a cluster of small sheds beside it. There's people in the dirt yard by a corral. Plus there's a sheriff's car parked alongside a couple of pickup trucks in front of the barn.

I swipe my cheeks dry. "Caspar's in big trouble, isn't he?"

"Yes. The sheriff's a Pinder too." Aunt Willie parks the truck and shoves her door open. "You probably better wait here."

"No way."

Aunt Willie tosses me a *thanks* look. We get out, meet up in front of the truck and walk side-by-side to the crowd. A tall, skinny man in blue jeans, a white T-shirt with the logo Wild Treks across his chest and a black hat cuts us off. I know from seeing him last night that it's Dirk's dad.

My aunt hooks an arm around my shoulders. "George, this is my nephew Gus Hart."

"Figured by the red hair he was kin to you," Dirk's dad says. He doesn't mention we already met.

Dirk doesn't either. But he shoots me a dagger look. I stretch tall as I can because that lets me look down my big Hart family nose at this mean-eyed kid.

Aunt Willie stands tall too and now works on shoving her long sleeves up past her elbows. "Calling the Sheriff is a bit much for a calf, isn't it?"

George Pinder looks out from under his hat's brim. "Turns out it's more than a calf, Doc."

"You going to explain what you mean or am I supposed to guess?"

Dirk puffs out his chest. "Your coyote killed one of our cows too."

"Over here." Dirk's dad leads the way to where a man in a sheriff's uniform is crouched down beside the body of a big, black cow with a bloody throat and belly.

"It happened this close to the house?"

"No. My men found the cow after I called you and used their horses to drag it back." Pinder points to the uniformed man. "That's when I called to report it."

The sheriff unfolds and stands up. "There's a three thousand dollar fine for setting wildlife loose on private property without the landowner's written permission."

Aunt Willie shakes her head. "Caspar was released into The Preserve."

The sheriff scratches his chin. "Releasing any wildlife in The Preserve would've had to be cleared with the local authority. That's me. Didn't happen."

"I didn't know about that law." Aunt Willie tucks straggling hair behind her ears. "But I'm going to need to study Caspar's radio collar data to believe he's been out of The Preserve attacking cattle on the Pinder ranch."

I spot something gray over by the corral and elbow my aunt.

"What?" She looks at me and then where I'm pointing at the coyote in a cage. "Caspar!"

Dirk's dad fingers his hat brim. "No need to bother with all that studying. My men saw that pesty coyote. Darted him and brought him back to the ranch. I'm happy to do away with him for you. Of course, if you want him for that menagerie you're running, I will expect to be paid for my cattle."

Aunt Willie's hands roll up into tight fists. "How much?"

"My cow was pedigree Black Angus. So I'll need five thousand dollars for her. Calf I'll let you have for fifteen hundred."

Aunt Willie's face goes red as her hair. "Get real. Besides, even if I believed Caspar killed the calf, which I don't, there is no way a lone coyote brought down a full-grown cow."

George Pinder rubs his chin. "There are teeth marks on the throat. That proves the coyote killed my cow."

Aunt Willie elbows past the men to reach the cow. Bends down to examine it.

"Look all you want. You're buying that cow."

"I won't pay you one red cent." Aunt Willie stands tall.

"No way! Huh, Dad," Dirk Pinder says.

I give Dirk the Jerk the evil eye.

Aunt Willie comes back alongside me. "Caspar didn't kill that cow."

The sheriff works at his chin with his hand. "But the bite marks on the cow's throat?"

Aunt Willie shakes her head. "The upper and lower jaw marks are too far apart and the teeth bite marks are too deep for Caspar's jaw size."

George Pinder's eyebrows pull tight together. "Then what killed my cow?"

"Panther!" I spit out.

SIXTEEN

"A Florida panther? Here?" The sheriff looks around like he's checking to see if one's sneaking up behind him.

I nod. "I saw one and it was big. I'll bet it killed that cow."

George Pinder glares at Aunt Willie. "What'd you do—import one of those cats? Set it loose on my land so you could study it?"

"Of course not." Aunt Willie faces me and grips my shoulders. "Where did you see a panther?"

"Close to Wahkullah House." I'm also going to tell about the cub in the cage trap but the sheriff speaks up.

"Did the boy say it was over by your place?"

I figure he didn't hear me clearly because Dirk Pinder is laughing real loud.

George Pinder whips his hat off and wipes his forehead with his shirtsleeve. "You better get your nephew out of the heat, Doc."

Aunt Willie's mouth opens like she's gonna say something. Instead, she grabs my arm and hustles me to the truck.

"I'll give you a week to pay up or that coyote's gonna be a pelt in my tourist shop," George Pinder calls as we climb into the truck.

When we're underway, I turn to my aunt. "Why'd you drag me away like a baby?"

Aunt Willie's frown is canyon deep. "Why'd you lie?"

"I didn't. I saw a Florida panther near Wahkullah House. Saw it—or maybe another one—over by Coop's." I sit up tall to settle my elbow on the edge of the open window just like she's doing. "And there was a mother panther with a cub last night near The Sisters."

Aunt Willie shakes her head. "Piling one lie on top of another doesn't make any of them true."

I stiffen up. Give her my meanest look. "It's all true! Why won't you believe me?"

Aunt Willie focuses on the road ahead. "I suppose you *think* you saw panthers."

"Why would I lie?"

Aunt Willie brakes so fast I've got to brace myself to keep from smacking the dash. "Because you do, don't you?"

She looks at me through the dust rolling in the open windows. "Your dad told me imagining things, like Daniel being with you, was how you coped with your brother's death. So he let you. Then you couldn't separate fact from fiction."

I crisscross fingers over my heart. "I saw panthers. I swear it."

She shoves the stick shift. The truck starts rolling again. "You need help—professional help. I think it is a good thing your dad's sending you to that school."

"You want to get rid of me too." I slide so close to the door the handle jabs my side. And just like that I grab it. Yank it. The door swings wide open.

"Gus!" Aunt Willie reaches for me. But I'm already out of the truck. Flying through hot air and dust.

The ground comes up fast. From a lifetime of gymnastics classes, I know to tuck and roll. The landing is a lot harder than tumbling onto a stack of mats. But I'm okay. I scramble to my feet. The pickup's trailing a thick tail of dust as it pulls off the road and stops.

I take off running. Jump over a skinny ditch. Plough through knee-high grass.

"Gus!"

I don't even look back. Pretty quick, I'm in a forest. Tall, straight-as-telephone-pole pines are everywhere. In between them, crooked smaller trees drip Spanish moss. And clusters of low bushes with giant fan-shaped leaves form a maze of pathways. I pick one, but the ground's slick with pine needles. I slide into a tree. Hug the trunk to keep from sprawling.

I can still hear Aunt Willie calling me. But she sounds far away, so she must have gone in a different direction. I wish she'd leave so I can go back to the road. I'll go to Coop's place. Doesn't matter it's a mess. I can hide there. Maybe I'll even find a place of my own and be a squatter like Coop.

Something slips through the shadows at my feet. It's a black snake bigger around than a garden hose. I take off running again.

After a while I have to slow down. Sticky mud is sucking at my feet. Sometimes, I sink in so deep the goo slips into my shoes. I'm sweating and swatting bugs by the time I'm back on solid ground.

Now things go from bad to worse.

While I'm hand-wiping mud off my legs, I discover two leeches.

"OOOOOH!"

The creepy creatures are black, about as long as my pinky finger, and stuck on my right leg between the bottom of my shorts and the top of my sock. I stomp my foot but the leeches don't fall off. "Yuck! Get off me!"

I try to pick one leech off. Shriek 'cause it's slimy and won't come off.

That's when Aunt Willie finds me.

"Gus! Thank heaven I heard you. And found you." She charges up all red-faced. "What in the world were you thinking running off? You could get so lost out here." Then she grabs me and hugs the breath out of me. "I couldn't stand it if anything happened to you. I don't want you to go. I swear."

"Aunt Willie."

"I mean it."

"Aunt Willie!"

She pushes me back enough to peer through her frizzy bangs at me. "What?"

I point at the black, pinky finger-sized things on my leg.

"Okay. Hold still." Aunt Willie crouches. Works her fingernail under one black leech until it drops off. She does the same with the other one. Then she straightens up again. "You are okay, aren't you? I mean besides the leeches and being dirty you are really all right." She finger wipes a glob of mud off my cheek. "

I nod. “Uh.” I have to clear my throat to push the words out. “I’m sorry.”

“Oh come here, you.” Aunt Willie hugs me again. “You don’t have to be sorry about making up that story about the panthers, but don’t do it again. I want you to always tell me the truth.”

“That was the truth. About seeing the panthers.” I push free and stiffen up. “I. Mean. Sorry. Daniel died.” My chin and lower lip jerk and my words come out jerky too. “On account of. Me.”

Aunt Willie’s eyes fill up with tears. “That just happened. It wasn’t your fault, kiddo.” She pushes my hair off my forehead. “I know you’ve been told that a bunch. Why won’t you believe it?”

“Because it *was* my fault. Daniel could’ve kept on running. He was the fastest sprinter on the track team. But he came back for me when I went after Grandpa’s guitar. Then the flash flood came. The water was so strong. It swept me away. And it was full of stuff. Daniel got me out. Then he was pushed under.”

My lower lip jerks so hard I have to bite it to stop it. Tears well and stream down my cheeks.

Aunt Willie uses her thumbs to mop them dry.

I spit out, “Let me stay with you. Please. I don’t want to go to that school. Or live there.”

Aunt Willie gives my cheeks another wipe. “I’ll talk to your dad about you staying with me.” She sighs real big. “But if he says you have to go, you have to go. Now, storm’s brewing. We better get back to the truck.”

She’s right about the storm, and sprinkles turn into a downpour before we’ve gone very far. That’s bad because it makes me remember the flash flood even though I try not to. I keep feeling like there's water sneaking up behind me. Even when I glance over my shoulder and don't see a wave, I remember the one that swept me off my feet. Rolled me over. Pulled me underwater.

"Hold it!" Aunt Willie hooks my arm and yanks me back to being with her. "There's cows over there."

I squint and look through the rain where she's pointing. There's a whole bunch of black cows. They look like the cow at the Pinders' place. Only these are alive and munching the grass growing in between the pines and palms.

"Grazing is illegal in The Preserve. These cows shouldn't be here," Aunt Willie says. "And I bet they belong to the Pinders. There's a brand on their rumps. Stay here. I'm going to try and get close enough to take a picture."

She tugs a cellphone out of her pocket and I wait, as ordered, while she eases up on the cows. Then I hear a throaty hiss and pivot toward the sound. Something's moving among a cluster of bushes.

"Aunt Willie!"

When she turns around, I point at the big yellow cat watching us with golden eyes.

SEVENTEEN

"See. I told you," I say as Aunt Willie starts up the truck.

She giggles. Then beams at me. "Oh my goodness! That was a panther. A Florida panther looked right at us and then slipped off into The Preserve. And we can't be more than two miles from Wahkullah House."

I nod. "Yeah. Cool."

"I have to admit I was scared for a minute because it looked so, well, *wild*." Aunt Willie giggles again. "But I think it was more afraid of us, well, you know, *people*, by the way it took off. Which, of course, is a good thing because there are people like the Pinders who do not want top predators like Florida panthers anywhere close to their livestock. Not that there should be cattle grazing in The Preserve."

Aunt Willie pauses only long enough to suck in a big breath. "And, although I'm totally guessing, I'd say that panther weighed about a hundred pounds so it was either a young male or it was a female. You really saw it, didn't you? I mean, I'm not hallucinating, right?"

"I saw it." I push my hands against the dash as we lurch forward and bounce onto the road. "I saw a panther the other times too. And the one last night had a cub."

"Yes. I believe you. I definitely, believe you. Why is this truck so slow?" Aunt Willie tromps the accelerator. "I've got to call the dean. I want you to tell him too. You're my witness. Okay?"

"Sure, but maybe you should wait. I mean Coop's rigging up his security cameras so they can be camera traps. To get you proof."

Aunt Willie nods. "He knows about the panther? Well, okay. Great idea. With photos the dean will have to renew my grant." She flips her hair back and tosses me a happy grin. "You know the panthers have only shown up since you got here. That makes you my lucky charm."

Me lucky? Maybe not for the panthers. "You don't think the Pinders would trap the cats, do you? Or shoot them? I mean Florida panthers are endangered so that would be against the law. Right?"

Aunt Willie harrumphs. "Pinders make their own laws on this island. But they might think twice if the public knows the panthers are here."

"You mean like posting photos on YouTube?"

"Brilliant!" Aunt Willie's grin becomes a full smile. "I meant telling the mainland TV station. But that's an even better idea. YouTube is national coverage. Global!"

We roll through the tunnel of trees and jerk to a stop in front of Wahkullah House. Coop is on the porch by the time we're climbing the steps. "Hurry up. I made chicken soup and you can eat while you tell Fiona and me what happened at the Pinder ranch."

Aunt Willie tips her head up and sniffs. "Ah, Coop, after living on my cooking, just the aroma of your chicken soup is a treat."

"So I can't wait. How'd it go with the Pinders?" Coop asks.

"Awful!" I tell him. "But then something good happened."

He looks curious but Aunt Willie says, "Over dinner."

Inside the kitchen, Fiona is setting a fourth steaming bowl of soup on the table. "Dad had to go out fishing. So I came back over and brought the biscuits I baked."

Coop leans down to whisper in my ear. "Consider yourself warned."

Fiona plants her hands on her hips. "I heard that."

Coop puts on a surprised look. "Heard what?"

Everyone sits down and I take the empty chair, which is between Coop and Fiona. The smell of the soup is making my mouth water and when Fiona passes me the plate of biscuits, I take one to be polite. When I bite down, the biscuit is as bad as her breakfast cookie but I make positive noises anyway.

Coop drums his fingers on the table. "Okay. Spill. All of it. What happened?"

Aunt Willie blots her lips with her napkin. "George claimed Caspar killed both his calf and a cow."

"Impossible!" Fiona says.

"Agreed. But he's caught Caspar and is threatening to kill him, if I don't pay nearly seven thousand dollars."

Coop groans. "I've only got six hundred saved up."

Fiona twists a lock of hair around her fingers. "But something else happened. I can feel it."

"You're right." Aunt Willie's smile pumps up her cheeks. "We went into The Preserve after we left the Pinders."

"How come?" Coop's eyebrows arch. "But more important I think there's an *and* coming."

Aunt Willie pokes me. "You tell, Gus."

"We found cows grazing in The Preserve."

Aunt Willie nods. "Too many to be strays. I took a photo of their brand. I'll bet when I check the county website that brand's registered to the Pinders."

"Serve them right if they get a fine." Fiona tucks her legs up under her on the chair.

"*And*." Aunt Willie hands slap a drumroll on the table. Then she points to me.

I say, "We saw a panther."

Fiona bounces. "No kidding?"

Coop's forehead pleats tight between his eyebrows. "You *both* saw one?"

Aunt Willie nods. "And Gus says you're already building camera traps for me. If I can prove there is at least one Florida panther on Pine Island, I can get my grant reinstated. *And* get conservation sanctions to protect the big cats. Maybe launch the reintroduction program to build up the population."

"You've got to do that," I say.

Coop's eyebrows arch. "So where do you figure this cat came from? I mean years of nothing and now?"

Aunt Willie finger-combs back her frizzy hair. "Sightings of panthers have been documented on the mainland as recently as eighteen months ago. I figure for some reason at least one swam the channel."

Coop strokes his cheek. "That's a pretty long swim."

Fiona shoves back from the table and carries dishes to the sink. "Clearly the panther didn't know our island is infested with Pinders. We definitely can't let the Pinders know about the panther."

Worry butterflies swarm in my belly. "There's something the Pinders already know."

Fiona meets my *we've got to tell look* and sighs. "Right, and we're really sorry."

Aunt Willie presses her fingers to her temples. "Now you're scaring me. What happened?"

EIGHTEEN

I lick my dry lips and start. "We took the tooth with us to The Sisters. I wanted to look at them. You know, through the hole. Thought that might be the clue we need to find Gasparilla's gold."

Fiona adds, "And it was a clue, wasn't it."

I shrug. "I looked through the hole in the tooth and saw some of the letters from the copper plate carved on the Sisters. Or at least I thought I did. We didn't have time to check it out. That's when the Pinders showed up, and I ran."

Fiona wiggles. "I hid to watch the Pinders when they got to The Sisters. But they went right on past. So I followed them."

My jaw drops. "I didn't know you did *that*."

She leans back to glare at me. "I'm not the one the Pinders caught."

My cheeks go flame hot. "Hey, if I hadn't found the trap and stayed to let the panther cub out, the Pinders would have caught it."

Fiona's face unscrunches. "Okay. That was good."

Aunt Willie lifts both hands. "So how did the Pinders get the tooth?"

I sag. "I laid it on the ground by the cage. Left it when Dirk's dad told Fiona and me to get out of there. I hoped they wouldn't see it. We went back for the tooth but it was gone."

Aunt Willie sighs. "So after missing out on finding the tooth at your house, Coop, the Pinders got lucky after all. And, with all Marcus knows about Pine Island, the Pinders probably now have all they need to find the treasure."

I choke out, "I'm sorry."

"Not so fast." Coop goes to the cupboard and comes back with the fat, pink pig cookie jar. Takes off the lid.

I shake my head when he places the cookie jar in front of me. "What? Is this like root beer floats? Things are bad so eat cookies?"

Coop shakes his head. "No. That's not what these cookies are good for."

Fiona peeks into the jar. "So that's where my breakfast cookies went."

Aunt Willie holds up her hand to refuse a cookie.

"Well, I'll have one." Coop's hand is so big he can only fit some of his fingers into the jar. And he pokes around like there's one special cookie he has to have.

"They're all the same," Fiona tells him.

"Not quite." When he's finally done digging, he pulls out the whale's tooth.

Willie takes it from him. Turns it over to examine the carvings. "How'd you get it back from the Pinders?"

"I didn't. You see, I made a number of models so I could study the tooth without any chance of damaging the carvings. This is the real one."

I lean across the table to point at the tooth. "But the Pinders still have the tooth map on the model."

"Nope." Coop winks his good eye at me. "I changed the pattern on each model by way of experimenting with what might fill in the gap on the map. The real tooth still has the gap."

"I missed that." I flop back in my chair.

Aunt Willie holds the tooth up for a close look. "Clever."

Coop's grin flashes his gold tooth. "Something made me decide I'd better hide the real tooth for a while."

Fiona leaps up and twirls around. "Thank you, Wahkullah House Spirit!"

I whoop. "Yes! Thank you!"

"So we've still got a chance to find the treasure." Aunt Willie lays the tooth on the table. "But, unless we can do that this week, I need another way to come up with money to keep the shelter going. It's going to take everything I've got in the bank—plus your savings, Coop—to rescue Caspar. That's assuming that the sheriff sides with the Pinders in claiming Caspar killed their cattle even after I prove he didn't. Oh!"

Aunt Willie's eyes pop open big and she presses both hands over her mouth.

Coop frowns. "What's the matter now?"

Aunt Willie lowers her hands to her lap. "It just hit me. I have to pay off the Pinders and let them believe Caspar's the culprit. If they know I know their cattle are in The Preserve and what really killed them, I'll be telling them about the Florida panther being there."

Fiona flops back down on her chair. "Whoa."

Coop shakes his head. "Can't do that. You know how George Pinder fought against even the possibility of reintroducing panthers to the island. You've got to rescue Caspar without making him suspicious. And we'll have to figure out some way to keep the shelter going until you get your grant reinstated."

I turn to Aunt Willie. "How about getting people to donate to the shelter?"

"I should have thought of that," Fiona says. "We'll set up a booth at the monthly market in the Square. It's only a week away and you don't have to register in advance. Just show up and pay twenty dollars. Bet, if I ask her, Mrs. James will even donate the twenty dollars. She loves coming out here to visit the shelter."

"Then that's Part A of our plan," Coop says. "We'll raise money to keep the shelter going first. That'll give us time for Part B, finding Gasparilla's gold."

"I'll bake cookies to sell at the market," Fiona volunteers.

"Gus can help me make jewelry." Coop looks at me. "And I know where I can borrow a guitar. Aunt Willie told me you play really well. People will always give something for a tune or two."

I shake my head. "I don't play anymore."

Truth is I haven't played a single chord since the night Daniel died.

"But you have to play, if that'll make money to take care of the animals." Fiona says. "And I'll sketch cartoon portraits. We each have to do what we can to raise money for the shelter."

My cheeks heat up again. "I'm *not* playing the guitar."

"Okay." Aunt Willie reaches across the table and squeezes my hand. "We'll figure out a way for you to help me on Market Day. I'll take along the raccoon kits and some other animals that aren't likely to be bothered by crowds to show people how their donations will help the island's wildlife."

Coop picks up the tooth and stuffs it back into the cookie jar. "For safekeeping until we're ready for another treasure hunt brainstorming session. Now, I'm going to go clean up the mess at my house and make camera traps. Because, beside finding pirate treasure, we've a panther to catch—digitally speaking."

"And I'll go talk to Mrs. James. Maybe she'll even give us something we can sell on Market Day. She knits really neat hats." Fiona hugs Aunt Willie and dashes out the door.

The minute they're both gone Aunt Willie hustles the dishes off the table. Piles them in the sink.

"I usually dry," I say.

Aunt Willie wipes her hands. "The dishes can wait. Before I go back to the university tomorrow, I've got maps and photos to look at. I want to think about the best places to put the camera traps. I also need to call George Pinder. I want to make sure he knows I'll be over in the morning to pay him and pick up Caspar."

She hurries to the hall but pauses in the doorway. "Don't worry, I'll call your dad later. Tell him I super *need* your help. And ask him to cancel coming here and to let you stay." She smiles. "That is if you're still sure you want to stay for the whole summer."

"Abso-total-lutely!"

"Okay, then." Her footsteps clomp to the back of the house.

I'm left alone in the kitchen. Well, me and a sink full of dirty dishes. I figure washing up is a way I can help out tonight. So I turn on the hot water, squirt blue dish soap over the entire mess and go to work.

When I tuck the last clean glass into its spot in the cupboard, I slide the dishtowel back over the oven handle and head upstairs. About halfway, I hear Aunt Willie talking and stop to listen. I think she must have called my dad. But she's saying stuff about forest canopy density and sun angles so I know she's talking to herself about setting up the camera traps. That's when I decide I'll call Dad myself.

Just thinking about doing that launches my worry butterflies again. What if Dad says I have to go to that summer school?

No. I won't. No way. Not before the end of the summer. I want to help take care of the animals at the shelter. They need me.

Once in my room, I sit on the window seat next to my duffel bag. Get my phone out. The light's pretty faded but there's enough to see outside. See The Preserve. I like how wild it looks. Makes me think there's safe places a mother panther and her cub can hide from the Pinders. And places where Gasparilla could have hidden his gold.

NINETEEN

To: brianhart@yahoo.com

Subject: See You Soon

Hey, Dad!

I'm glad you're coming for Market Day this weekend. Only I've got a favor to ask. I know you told Aunt Willie I've got go to that summer school. Even though I REALLY don't want to. But it doesn't start for two weeks. So can I please stay here an extra week. PLEASE!

Caspar—you know the coyote Aunt Willie rescued from the Pinders—is going to go live at The Nature Center in Asheville, NC. I've been taking care of him since he came back here. Coop made him the only guest I take care of. I feed him. Clean up his cabin. Talk to him. Aunt Willie says it's because of me that Caspar has calmed down again and acts okay around people again. And that's how come he gets to go to The Nature Center to live. So I really want to be here until he goes. Can I please stay just one more week?

Love you!

Gus ☺

I chew on my lip reading over my email. Add one more *PLEASE* at the end. Then puff out a big bunch of hope as I push *send*.

Three more days until Dad arrives. Five more days until I have to leave. Unless Dad gives in. Still, that will only get me one extra week here.

So I've got two weeks tops to find Gasparilla's gold and become a hero. Then maybe Dad won't send me to live at that school.

What would also be cool before I leave is for the camera traps to get pictures of the Florida panther. Then Aunt Willie can get her grant back. But so far there've been no panthers in any of the pictures the cameras snapped. There's been deer and boar. Twice there were foxes. Aunt Willie's worried the panther has gone back to the mainland. Coop said he doesn't think so since it has a little cub. Then I heard Aunt Willie say, *But nobody's seen the cub except Gus.*

While I wait for Dad to answer my email, I fold a piece of paper. Do origami the way Coop taught me to make a bird. It turns out perfect on the first try. I sail the bird across the kitchen and go get it.

Dad still hasn't answered.

He must not be online. I close the laptop. Get up from the table. Figure I'll take Caspar a couple of the meatballs Coop's made for tonight's dinner.

When I open the refrigerator, one of the papers taped to the door flies off. It floats—cross my heart—across the kitchen. Lands below a big blow-up photo Coop made of The Sisters. And the paper that came off the refrigerator is a picture of the whale's tooth with the hole circled.

Whoa! "Wahkullah House Spirit, are you telling me something?"

I hold my breath and listen. All I hear is the clock in the hall ticking. And my heart thumping. But right as I take a breath Fiona comes in.

Her face scrunches up when our eyes meet. "What's going on?"

"We've got to go to The Sisters."

"Now?"

"Now! In fact, we should have done this already. Checked it out." I dash to the cookie jar and pull out the tooth.

"What are you talking about?"

"I saw some of the letters from the copper plate code carved on The Sisters. What does that mean? And are more of the letters from the code carved there too?"

"I'll get the printout of the copper plate code." Fiona runs to the refrigerator.

And on the photo of the tooth, I write a note for Coop. *Gone to The Sisters. Be back fast. Promise.*

Fiona sets the cookie jar on the corner of the note. Grabs a flashlight out of the drawer. "It's only just after six so it won't be dark for a while. Still, better safe than sorry. Why haven't we already checked this out?"

"We got crazy busy getting ready for Market Day." I shut the kitchen door behind us and hustle down the steps.

We walk fast. I hold the tooth hugged against me, like I'm carrying a football. Feel like I'm on my way to scoring a touchdown. I'm so full of hope I'm about to pop.

By the time we reach The Sisters, the sun is sinking below the tops of the tall palms and the shadows are buzzing with bugs. There's also lots of creepy shadows. Hiding places for snakes. Scorpions. Spiders. Who knows what else. But I ignore all of that and focus on The Sisters.

Not just because they're shimmering in the shadows. I'm looking for the clusters of letters I saw before. I hold up the tooth and look through it like I did that night. "Hey, it was moonlight then. Shine the flashlight on The Sisters, will you."

Fiona does and I look. Really hard. But there's a lot of bits of seashell to see plus there's a lot stuff carved into the coquina: initials, dates, names and even symbols like hearts and a lightning bolt.

"Gus." Fiona pokes me.

"Hey." I hold out the tooth to hand it to her. "You want to look for the treasure clues?"

She doesn't take the tooth. Taps her finger to her lips and whispers, "I heard something."

TWENTY

Dirk Pinder bursts through the bushes and his flashlight beam smacks me in the face. Even nearly blinded, I can see his mean frown. He spits out, “You!”

His dad George Pinder is right behind him. “Seems like every time we go looking for strays we find you two on our land.”

Fiona plants her hands on her hips. “The Preserve is public land.”

George Pinder looks straight at me. “So you think there’s a treasure buried around here, huh? Tell me where you think it is.”

I’m about to say *no way* when I see George Pinder is holding a rifle. My heart leaps so hard it’s a wonder it stays in my chest.

Dirk points. “They’re out here nosing around The Sisters again, Daddy.”

George strolls over to one of the spires. “Ah yes. The Sisters. Carved my initials on this one the year I graduated high school.” He pats the rock. “Tell me more about what The Sisters have to do with a treasure. And how come every time I find you out here you’ve got another whale’s tooth?”

I need a lie.

A good one.

Before I can think one up there's a rustling noise. Then a shadow comes to life and leaps out of the dark. George Pinder raises his rifle. Fires.

CRACK!

I drop to the ground. Drop the whale's tooth. Then push up fast to see if Fiona's okay. She is. But there's a big yellow cat—a Florida panther--stretched out at the base of The Sisters. It's spitting and snarling and trying to get up too. Only it can't. Its side is all dark and wet with blood.

Fiona gasps. Clamps both hands over her mouth.

My stomach cramps. Tears flood my eyes.

Dirk backs up until he bumps into me. "Kill it, Daddy."

"No!" I shout and scramble up.

Fiona throws herself at George Pinder as he takes aim at the cat on the ground.

"Get her off me."

Dirk drops the flashlight to grab Fiona. I charge him but don't get there fast enough.

BANG!

The big cat goes quiet.

Lies still.

I stare at the panther through hot tears.

It's dead. I know it.

Just like I knew Daniel was dead, though it was two days before they found him.

George Pinder nudges the cat with the toe of his boot. "There's one less critter to bother my cows."

"Good going, Daddy." Dirk's all smiles until Fiona wrestles free of his grip. She plucks the flashlight off the ground and aims it at the dead cat.

"I'll tell. Florida panthers are protected by law."

"No law should keep a rancher from protecting his livestock." George Pinder shoves his hat back and looks down his nose at her. "Besides, it won't matter if you tell. Who's going to believe you when they can't find the panther? Which they won't, because I practice the three "S's: shoot, shovel and shut up."

Fiona bristles. "I'll tell anyway."

George Pinder goes toe-to-toe with her. "Not if you know what's good for you and yours."

I square my shoulders. "I'll tell too."

Fiona beams at me.

George Pinder gives me a look hot enough to toast marshmallows. "You do and I'll rain a storm of trouble on Doc Hart. My cousin's the judge and can easily find a reason to cancel her permit to run a wild animal shelter at Wahkullah House."

I'm sure it's true and I feel like I'm shrinking. Besides, there's a sound. A shrill chirp. It's coming from one of The Sisters.

Dirk's face scrunches. "Hey. What's that?"

I wonder too when whatever's doing it chirps again. Then an animal crawls out of a hole at the base of that Sister. It's a golden-yellow and brown spotted panther cub. I'm guessing it's the one I let out of the cage trap. It looks up at me with big blue eyes and a kitten-sweet face. Then it races to the body on the ground, head butts it, and chirps a cry I feel to my bones.

Fiona shines the flashlight on it. "You killed its mama."

"And I'll put it out of its misery." George Pinder takes aim at the cub and quick as a blink I slam into him.

BANG!

The gunshot's blast is like being inside thunder. Dirk's dad is already shoving me away before we land on the ground. "Get off me!" He scrambles to reach the rifle he dropped.

I wrap my legs around his legs. Grab handfuls of his shirt and hang on like one of those leeches that were stuck on me. But he's stronger. I lose my grip. End up on my back when he stands up. I scoot away from his kick.

George Pinder hollers, "Use your knife, son. Finish the cat!"

"NO!" Fiona and I duet.

Dirk hesitates. The panther cub yowls. Darts away.

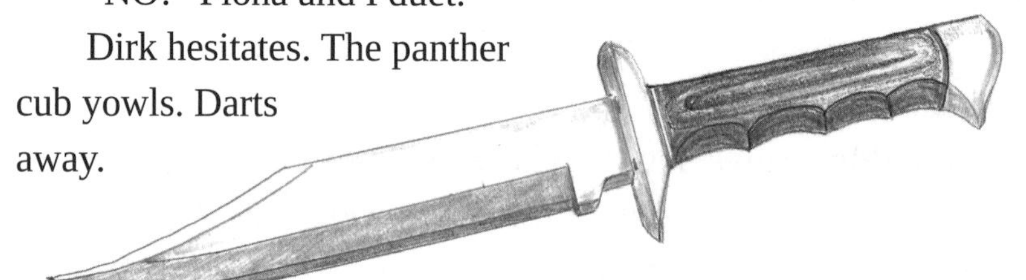

Dirk throws his knife. It slices the air. Bounces off one of The Sisters and stabs the shadows. Meanwhile, the cat disappears, crashing into the brush.

George Pinder and I get up. Eye each other. Then he retrieves the knife and hands it back to his son. "You need to man up, son."

My ears go hot. "Why do you want to kill it? Why'd you shoot its mother?"

"Told you—because it's a threat to my cattle." George Pinder gives a disgusted grunt. "Don't matter that we didn't get the cub. It's too little to make it without its mama."

Then George Pinder is right in front of me giving me a beady-eyed glare. “And if you happen to find a treasure, boy, remember who owns everything on this land.” He turns to Fiona. “And you remember your dad fishes on my nephew’s boat. Got it?”

Fiona nods but I see her crossing her fingers behind her back.

George Pinder nudges Dirk’s shoulder. “Let’s go get us some shovels out of the truck. Get this cat buried where it won’t be found.” With an over-the-shoulder glance at Fiona and me he adds, “Y’all be gone when we get back.”

The Pinders leave The Sisters the way they came in. Then Fiona and I rush over to the big cat on the ground. I crouch down for a closer look. Hold my fingers in front of her nose. “She’s really dead.”

“Take a picture with your cell phone.”

“Can’t. Left it in my room.”

She huffs out a breath. “We’ll tell Coop what happened. He’ll believe us. And he’ll know what to do.”

“We can’t tell.” I straighten up. “You heard what he said about Aunt Willie losing her permit. Your Dad works for his nephew. *And* Coop’s a squatter on Pinder land. Remember?”

Fiona stamps her foot. “Well, we have to do something.”

“Right.” I pick up the whale’s tooth. “We’ve got to rescue that cub.”

TWENTY-ONE

"I saw something. There. Gimme the flashlight." I take it from her and aim the beam. Spotlight a fat raccoon's rump retreating under a bush. I give Fiona a *sorry* look and hand the flashlight back.

"Well, the panther cub has to be here. Somewhere." Fiona fans bugs away from her face with her free hand while she scours the ground with the light.

I examine the puzzle of shadows cast by the moonlight sifting through the palms. "But where?"

Worry crinkles Fiona's forehead. "George Pinder's right. The cub's too young to be on its own. We've got to find it."

"Right." I pivot slowly. Look hard.

"Look up, dodos."

I jump at that voice. Get a belly cramp at the sight of Dirk Pinder marching toward us.

"Go away!" Fiona blasts him with the flashlight beam.

His face scrunches in the glaring light but he stays. Points skyward. "Look up!"

Fiona doesn't lift the flashlight but looks. "At what?"

"There!" Dirk grabs her wrist to direct the light at one big tree branch.

"Let go of me." Fiona jerks free. Then she aims the light and gasps, "There it is!"

The panther cub is crouched on a branch with its rear against the tree's trunk. It looks back at us with scared eyes.

Then I see something else that's gleaming in the moonlight. Dirk the Jerk's holding a rifle. Fiona must see it too. Just like that, she raises the flashlight like she's ready to fight. I dash to her side.

"Cool it. This is only a tranquilizer gun." Dirk's chin juts out with his pout. "Lucky I brought it and know how to use it. It's how we're gonna get that wild cat down. Unless one of you wants to climb the tree and grab it."

Fiona lowers the flashlight. "Won't the fall hurt it?"

"Naw." Dirk hoists the rifle and fidgets with it. "The branch isn't that high."

I don't like the way Fiona's looking at Dirk. Like she trusts him a little. Well, I don't. "So where's your dad?"

"Burying the big cat." Dirk pulls a silver dart out of his pocket and shoves it into the gun. "Dad sent me to *stalk* you two. Find out if you really know where there's a buried treasure."

"And he sent you with a tranquilizer gun?" I put on my mean face, which is easy to do looking at him. "You suppose to knock us out?"

"No, stupid." His eyebrows arch. "I'm manning up, my way. Just hope he doesn't catch me."

Now Fiona smiles like she's impressed, a little bit.

I *really* don't like that. "You know how to use that gun?"

"Said I did, didn't I? We use it to catch deer to pen up for the tourists. Now get outta my way." Dirk elbows past me and takes aim.

"Wait!" Fiona grabs his arm. "That cub's littler than a deer. You sure the tranquilizer won't kill it?"

"Trust me."

She lets go of his arm like she is trusting him. So I hip bump him.

"Hey, fart face." Dirk shoves me back. "I've only got one dart."

Fiona bounces between us. But it's me she looks in the eye. "We don't have a choice."

That's when I look up again and see the empty branch. "Hey, it's gone!"

"Can't be far." Fiona dashes in one direction.

I go in another. "Do you see it?"

"Not yet."

I drop down on my hands and knees to peer under some low bushes. Hope to see the cub. Hope it doesn't bite me. Definitely hope not to find any snakes. "It's not here."

"Shh," Dirk hisses. "Listen!"

All three of us freeze like statues. Me—I rock back on my heels, cradle the whale's tooth and hold my breath to listen really hard. I don't hear anything. Well, nothing but the soft papery sound of leaves in the breeze. And yet there's something close by. I'm sure of it because the hair on the back of my neck is prickling.

POOF!

The sound of the tranquilizer gun firing makes me jump to my feet just in time to catch a glimpse of the panther cub. It leaps past me with a silver dart sticking out of its front shoulder.

"C'mon." Dirk takes off. "We can't lose it."

Fiona's so fast she soon takes the lead. And she's got the flashlight.

Bringing up the rear, I run as fast as I can through the dark. And we keep on chasing after that cub for like ever. I chug up alongside Dirk. "I thought that dart's supposed to put it to sleep?"

Dirk's bony elbow jabs my side. "Takes time."

I elbow him right back. "How long?"

"Over here."

Dirk and I race to where Fiona's crouched down over the cub. "It's breathing okay."

Dirk whistles.

"What? You didn't know it would be?"

Dirk gives me a dirty look.

"Uh oh," Fiona groans. "There's some blood on its hip. It's wounded. We need to get it to Wahkullah House. Coop'll know how to take care of it. Or he'll take it to the vet." She stands up and snatches the gun from Dirk. "I'll carry this."

"No way!"

Fiona cradles the gun in her arms. "I'm carrying it because you're going to have to carry the cub all the way to Wahkullah House."

"Me?"

"Of course you." Fiona smiles at him. "You're bigger and stronger than either of us."

I bristle. "He's not stronger than me." But that's pretty sure a lie because Dirk Pinder has bulging muscles where I've just got arms. Then I prove I'm lying because I hand Fiona the whale's tooth and try to pick up the cub. It's heavier than I thought it was. Besides, asleep it's all stretched out. And it's floppy. So right away one end is slipping out of my arms.

"Really?" Fiona divides a look between us. "You two will have to carry it together."

Dirk grumbles but lifts the cub's back end. I pick up the front and walk alongside him with the panther between us. Fiona leads but keeps stopping to let us catch up.

"Can't you go any faster?" She asks after a bit.

Dirk and I exchange *gimme a break* looks. He stops. "How about we take a breather and you go see if we're close."

"Works for me." I lower my end of the cub to the ground as Dirk lowers his.

When Fiona trots off, Dirk sits down on a fallen tree trunk. I sit next to him only because it's there or the ground. I work on rubbing my aching arms and ignore him until I can't.

"Hey. Carrot hair. You really think there's pirate treasure out by The Sisters?"

I look down my nose at him. Don't say anything.

He grunts. "Yeah, well, I'm going to tell my dad you think there's treasure buried on the beach. He'll have his men dig up every inch. Turtles' nests too."

I ball my hands into fists. "You wouldn't!"

"Will." Dirk's grin shoves his cheeks so high his eyes squint. "Or you can tell me about the treasure. What do you know?"

I chew on my lip trying to figure out what to tell him.

Dirk shrugs. "Whatever."

I sit up straighter. "Okay. We know you know about the whale's tooth map. But you don't have the real tooth. Just a model Coop made. We've got the real tooth. Only we don't know where the treasure is buried."

Dirk's face scrunches up like he doesn't trust me but he also doesn't know what to make of what I told him.

Daniel always says, *When you don't know what to say tell the truth*. I roll my lips in tight to my teeth to hide my smile. Right then, the cub's ears twitch and I leap up. So does Dirk the Jerk.

"Uh oh. We better get moving before it wakes up." I pick up my end of the cub and he hoists his. But Dirk's not ready to let go of picking at me about the treasure. Starts again once we're walking.

"So why do you keep going back to The Sisters?"

"There you are." Fiona's arrival saves me from having to answer. "It's not much farther. And I brought help."

She shines the light where the brush is swaying and parting. I'm expecting Coop. But it isn't him.

"Dad?"

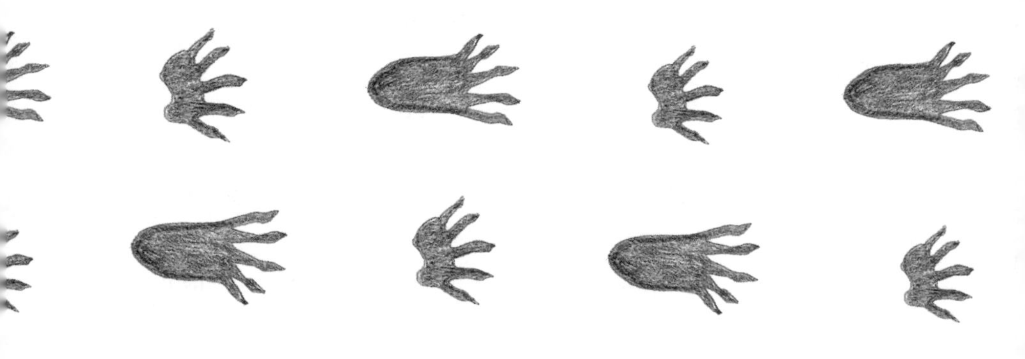

TWENTY-TWO

"You sure this little male was alone?" Coop strokes the head of the sedated panther cub.

I nod. "Only saw one cub with its mother at the cage trap. And again tonight."

Fiona digs scissors and a roll of bandaging tape out of a drawer. "I didn't hear more than one."

"Well, okay. There probably is just one cub then." With that Coop goes to work tending its wound.

I lean in close. "Will it be okay?"

Fiona elbows me. "Don't jinx it."

Coop says, "Luckily, the cut's not deep. It won't need stitches."

"So there, jerk." Dirk punches my shoulder before biting into an apple.

"You're the jerk." Fiona reaches around me and snatches the apple. "That food's for the *animals*."

Dirk's lower lip pokes out with his pout. "Hey, I'm hungry as a bear."

He trails Fiona to the fridge. After the refrigerator door swooshes open and shut, the only sound is the click-snap of the scissors and the wind rubbing a branch against the window. We're in one of the cabins at Wahkullah House but this one isn't anything special. Just a workroom with boxes and giant bags heaped high as the window's ledge. Plus the gray-topped table with chrome legs where the panther cub is stretched out.

I stand, statue-still, watching Coop work until a strong hand grips my shoulder. I jerk in surprise. My pounding heart drops right down to the pit of my stomach, when I look over my shoulder. Dad's wearing his *this is serious* look. He head nods me to follow him outside.

There, in the dark beyond the bright light streaming through the screen door, he leans close and talks real low. "I got your email when my plane landed. I'm sorry, son, but there's no way you can stay the extra week. We're leaving in two days, right after Market Day."

"You came here just to make sure I go to that school?"

Dad frowns. "No. I also came to help out my sister."

"With Market Day."

"Sure, since I'm here, but I'm co-signing a loan to make sure she can keep her home."

"And the shelter."

Dad shakes his head. "Keeping that going is another matter entirely."

"But we've got to. For the animals." I spread my arms to make my plea. "And I've got to stay for the whole summer. I just have to."

Dad's forehead develops Grand Canyon creases. "You called me the day after you got here because you wanted to leave right then. Now you keep begging to stay. You want to explain to me what's changed?"

What do I tell him? It's Fiona. Saving the turtle nests. Coop's root beer floats. Aunt Willie coming after me when I ran away. Trying to figure out where to find pirate treasure. Helping Caspar. Rescuing the panther cub.

"Well?"

I point at the cabin screen door. Through it I can see everyone inside huddled around the panther cub. "They need me."

Dad's eyebrows skyrocket. "To do what?"

The tone in his voice stabs me. Why is it so hard to believe anyone would need me? Because I'm not Daniel?

I blink fast to clear away the tears blurring my vision.

"Look," Dad says. "I think the school I found in Seattle is what *you* need. I'll even spring for guitar lessons. I know you really took to playing when Gramps was teaching you. He tried to teach me when I was your age but music wasn't my thing."

I shake my head. "I'm never touching a guitar again.

Dad sighs. "Well, you can always change your mind."

"I did. So let me stay here for the summer. Please!"

"No." Dad's shoulders sag like he's really tired. "You're going to that school. It's what's best for you. Understand?"

I understand I've only got through this weekend to figure out a way to stay for the rest of the summer.

TWENTY-THREE

The two days left before Market Day are crazy. Dad pitches in. He even helps feed the guests and clean up their cabins. Meanwhile, I help Coop build toys to sell. They're made out of junk, but they look like cool alien creatures. Some of them even walk or crawl when you wind them up. Plus we built a small version of one of his Beatles to draw people to our booth. Fiona spends most of the day in Aunt Willie's kitchen baking animal cookies. They're supposed to be sugar cookies in the shape of animals at the shelter. There are skunk cookies, alligator cookies, pelican cookies and panther cub cookies. Oh, and turtle cookies for good measure. Honest

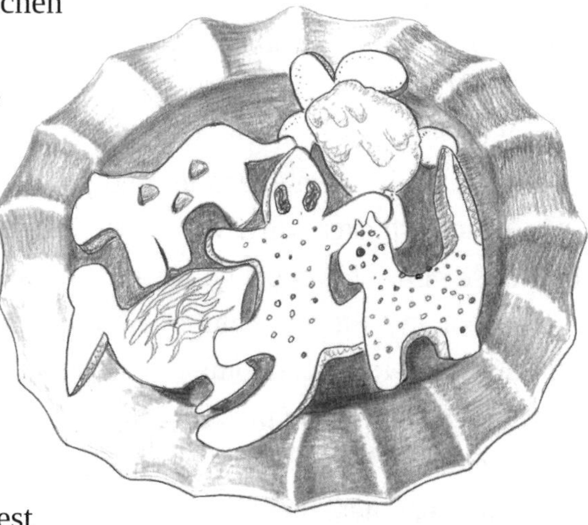

truth—and she made us sample each kind—they all taste just like her breakfast cookies. *Awful!* But I don't tell her that.

As soon as Aunt Willie gets home, Coop and I take her to see our newest guest. Her eyes pop. "Oh my gosh. A panther cub." She divides a look between us. "Why didn't you call me? What in the world? I mean how? Where?"

I spill the whole story. When I get to the part about George Pinder shooting the mother panther, her eyes tear up.

"Oh my goodness. That's terrible. I get that ranchers want to protect their cattle from predators, but the Pinders have no right grazing their cattle in The Preserve. And do you know there are fewer than one hundred Florida panthers left? I mean imagine you're in a room with one hundred people. And that's all the people left in the whole world."

Coop looks as amazed as I feel.

Then Aunt Willie crouches down to get a good look at the cub in the big box cage that Coop built for it. This is only its temporary home while he works on creating a guest house especially for it.

"Well, it doesn't seem bothered that we're here."

"Probably because we've been feeding it," I say.

Aunt Willie straightens up and points at the cub. "So there's Pine Island's poster baby. We'll take him along on Market Day to introduce him. This cub's going to help me convince the university to sponsor my Florida panther reintroduction program. And that will draw eco-tourists hoping to photograph a wild Florida panther, which is bound to be a plus for the local economy."

She plants her hands on her hips. "The Pinders won't dare trap or kill any panthers then."

"Cool!" I high five Coop.

Aunt Willie high fives me too. "Now let's finish getting ready to make money for the shelter. I'm going to go whip up two batches of fudge: one chocolate and one butterscotch." She winks at me. "Just in case Fiona's cookies need a little assist at the bakery table."

Saturday—Market Day—arrives sunny but not steamy hot. In other words, perfect.

And wow!

There's like a zillion people that come by our booth. Everybody wants to see the animals, especially the panther cub. It doesn't seem bothered by all the attention at all and mostly naps. Meanwhile, people *ooh and ahh.* Lots also pay a dollar to suggest a name for the cub. As each entry goes into the special box Coop made, it plays the cub's chirp. Which is totally cool!

Meanwhile, Coop's also selling his toys and the necklaces he made out of seashells and beads. Fiona's set up an easel to do portraits. Dad's cooking hotdogs, which are really popular. Me—I'm in charge of selling cookies and fudge. So once the fudge goes I'm not very busy. That's okay with me. I'm working on how I'm going to convince Dad I shouldn't leave with him tonight. So far, here's what I've come up with:

1. The cub won't eat if I'm not here. (Not true. Dad will know that.)

2. Coop and Fiona can't take care of the animals without me. (Not true. Dad will know that.)

3. I'm happier than I've been since Daniel died. (True. Dad won't get that.)

"Excuse me, dearie."

I blink. Come back to my job at the bakery table. See there's a chubby woman stuffing Fiona's animal cookies into her backpack.

"No. Stop!" I yank the cookie tray off the table and out of her reach.

"Don't worry. I'm buying them." Smiling, she takes hold of the other end of the cookie tray and tugs. "It's for a good cause. The wildlife shelter."

I tug even harder. "But these cookies are—uh—filling. You don't want them all!"

"It's all right." The chubby woman lets go. Leaves me holding the tray while she picks cookies off it. "I know Fiona baked these, dearie. My Ralphie loves her cookies."

Fiona in a red dress and a big sun hat dashes over to hug the woman. "Mrs. James, I knew you'd come. Where's Ralphie?"

Mrs. James drops the last cookie into her backpack. "I couldn't bring him, sweetie. You know how he loves to chase things."

Relief floods through me. "Oh, I get it, Ralphie's a dog."

Mrs. James pays for the cookies and also drops a twenty-dollar bill into the donation bucket. "My Ralphie's a black lab. He'll be one year old next week and Fiona's cookies will be his birthday present."

Once Mrs. James marches away, Fiona sighs. "Everyone's section is a success but mine. No one wants to sit for a sketch."

It's true. I've watched her trying to coax people to have a seat next to her easel.

"Wait. I've got an idea." Fiona ducks down and hauls out the battered leather case tucked underneath the bakery table. It's the guitar Coop brought along.

I hold up both hands. "Forget it."

Fiona gives me a pout. "Please. Come play next to my easel." She lays the case on the table. Pops it open. "Music will make people want to sit and listen. While they're sitting, I can draw their cartoon portraits and they'll buy my sketches."

When Fiona takes the guitar out and shoves it into my arms, I'm instantly sick to my stomach. I flash back to playing my guitar that night at camp. The night of the flash flood.

I lay the guitar back in its case. "Can't. Sorry."

Fiona's face pinches and she opens her mouth like she's about to give me what for. Then Dirk Pinder charges up. Blurts out. "I told my dad. I wasn't going to because you're—well—okay. Only I had to tell him. I didn't have a choice. So I had to warn you."

I aim daggers at Dirk. "What'd you tell?"

"That you have the real tooth map and you've figured it out."

"You told him *that*?" Fiona flat-hand shoves me.

I poke Dirk. "I never told you we figured out the map. We haven't."

Dirk holds up both hands. "Hey. He threatened to sell my horse. So I stretched the truth a little. Don't you do that, when you have to?"

I'm too upset to speak.

Fiona's not. She plants her hands on her hips and spits out, "You are such jerks. Both of you."

I try to say, *It wasn't me*. All that comes out is a *croak*.

Dirk's cheeks pink up. "Hey, I came to warn you. And I heard Dad call Uncle Marcus. He told him, *The only way to get what we want is to take something they want.*"

I clear my throat and push the words out. "We've got to warn Coop."

"I'll do it." Fiona dashes for his side of our booth.

Dirk starts to follow her but I snag his arm. "How come you're helping us?"

Dirk yanks free. "You don't trust me?"

"Nope."

Then Fiona's back. Tells me, "Coop's gone. Your dad said he went to meet somebody at his van."

Just like that, I'm scared for Coop. "This could be a trick."

I take off for the field where everyone parked this morning. Fiona's right beside me. And, to my surprise, Dirk is too. The three of us charge between the rows of cars and vans and pickup trucks. I spy Coop's white panel van as the brown car parked in front of it starts up.

"Watch out!" Dirk shoves Fiona to get her out of the way. The brown car shoots past, spraying gravel. Then it's gone and I hear a moan.

"Coop?" I reach the van as the side panel slides open.

TWENTY-FOUR

Coop sits on the edge of the open van, pressing his fingers to a bloody gash on his head. "I can't believe it."

"I'll get something for that." Fiona climbs past him and into the van.

I swing up to sit next to Coop. "What happened?"

"Marcus Pinder hit me." Coop presses the paper napkins Fiona hands him to the wound.

"Uncle Marcus hit you?" Dirk's eyes and mouth go big and round.

Fiona sits down on the other side of Coop. "Scrawny old Marcus Pinder beat you up?"

Coop pats his temple. "He hit me from behind is what he did. But I deserve it. I've been an idiot." His face sags.

"Marcus called me this morning. Said he knew about the whale's tooth map. That, if I'd show him the real whale's tooth, he'd share what he knows about Pine Island and its history. He was sure together we could figure out where Gasparilla buried his gold. And we could all go fifty-fifty on the treasure. I wanted to be a hero so I brought the tooth. I was looking at something he pointed out when he smacked me with my own coffee thermos. And stole the tooth."

My jaw drops. "You brought the tooth here?"

Coop points at Dirk. "What are you doing here? You're a Pinder."

Fiona shrugs. "He came to warn us there could be trouble."

Right then fire sirens wail and get louder, like they're getting closer. "Look!" I point at the smoke billowing up from the Market Day tents.

This time there's four of us running because Coop comes along. But going in this direction is harder. The crowd's flooding into the parking lot. Fleeing whatever trouble is happening. We have to weave between all of the people. But we do until, finally, we're back at our booth.

Now, the fire truck's there too. So is the sheriff's car. Firemen in full gear are spraying foam on Coop's side of the booth. The sheriff is talking to Aunt Willie and Dad where they're huddled in the center of a cluster of animal cages. Fiona and Coop push into that circle. Dirk runs off.

Dad tells the sheriff, "A table was overturned. I was picking stuff up when somebody screamed. I turned around and saw the barbeque on the ground and the grass on fire."

The sheriff leaves right after that. And Coop says, "I'll bet all this—even getting me to bring the whale's tooth—was a trick. The Pinders' way of causing more problems for us."

"Phooey!" Fiona stamps her foot.

I feel my face scrunch up mean as it gets. “But why’d you bring the real tooth, Coop?”

“I didn’t. How could you think I would?”

My cheeks go flame hot as I meet Coop’s hard look.

“Stop!” Aunt Willie’s cheeks are tear-streaked. “We can’t let the Pinders divide us. We’ve got to stick together. Figure out what to do together because *someone* stole from us.”

Fiona gasps, “The donations!”

Aunt Willie holds up a plastic bag full of money. “No. Not that.”

My heart thumps my ribs because I’m scared I know what’s gone. “Did they take the cub?”

TWENTY-FIVE

Back at Wahkullah House, I help Coop lift the animals in their cages out of his van. And say, "We've got to figure out how to get the cub back from the Pinders."

Dad says, "That's the sheriff's job. *If* the Pinders are the ones who stole it. You don't know that for a fact."

The rest of us exchange *yes we do* looks.

Fiona marches past with her arms full of Market Day stuff. "Who else would?"

"I agree, but I still don't get why?" Aunt Willie hands me bags to carry inside. 'They can't possibly believe I've got enough money to ransom the cub."

Coop's gold tooth gleams in his frown. "I think they believe we know where to find Gasparilla's gold."

"But we don't." Fiona's ponytail whips with her head shake.

My swallow ripples down my throat. "You don't think they'll hurt the cub, do you?"

Aunt Willie's face goes as red as her hair. "They wouldn't dare."

"I for one don't trust a Pinder any way, any how." Coop takes us all in with one look. "For sure, they know we'd do anything to protect that little guy."

Heat floods my cheeks. "We've got to rescue the cub."

"Like I said before, that's the sheriff's job," Dad says.

I say, "But the sheriff's a Pinder too."

Dad says, "I'm sure he's the sheriff first. Now, go get your bag. We have a plane to catch."

Fiona and I share a *this is terrible* look as we carry our loads into the kitchen. She flips back her ponytail. "I'll email you as soon as the cub's back home safe."

If it's safe.

Dad's voice booms from outside. "Hurry up, Gus."

It's not fair that I have to leave right now. I'm so angry and sad at once I feel like I'll explode. Fiona makes it even worse by slipping up so close our hands bump.

She says, "This is the pits. You should be here when the cub's rescued. And help us hunt for Gasparilla's gold."

Abso-total-lutely!

"Gus! Get a move on!"

Fiona rolls her eyes. I start to say what I'm thinking but the words wad up. Stick in my throat. I march upstairs and past the grandfather clock to my room. Shut the door. And lean against it before I can finally let the words out. "It's not fair. It's not fair! It's NOT fair!"

But I haven't got a choice.

I cross the room to the window seat. Snatch up my duffel.

I hear the screen door bang. "Hustle up, Gus!" Dad calls from downstairs.

I look out the window. At The Preserve all washed in sunset gold and heaped full of shadows. There's something so beautiful about what I see it makes my breath catch. And I wonder if there are more panthers out there. Then I think about the cub. And how George Pinder shot its mother. What's he going to do to the cub?

I can't go!

I've got to get the cub away from the Pinders.

I drop my duffel and lift the window. Lean out into the hot breeze. It's pretty far down to the ground. But there's a trellis running up the side of the house and it's within reach. I grab it and give it a shake. I think it'll hold me.

On the count of three, I think. And, so I don't chicken out, I leap for the trellis on *two*.

TWENTY-SIX

The trellis jiggles against the side of the house. I look down and my stomach drops to my toes.

What was I thinking? I'm scared of heights. And it is way far down to the ground. I stretch to reach the window ledge and climb back inside.

"Let's go! Do you hear me?" Dad calls from somewhere downstairs.

A fresh dose of *no way* steadies me. I ease down another rung on the trellis. And another.

The trick, I decide, is not to look down. Doesn't matter that I'm sweating. Or that my mouth is as dry as one of Fiona's cookies.

GASP! The next trellis rung snaps under me. I grab tight. Find a place for my foot.

"Gus?"

I look up at Fiona leaning out the window, looking down at me. I try to call out that I'm okay but only manage to gulp air.

"Hang tight. I'll get help."

She vanishes. Did she go to tell my dad? I know what he'll do. He'll get a ladder and rescue me. Relief floods through me but drains away just as fast.

I don't want to be rescued. Because then I'll have to go to the airport. Go to Seattle. Go to that school. And I won't be able to help the panther cub. Or hunt for Gasparilla's gold.

Right then is when I see what I didn't notice before. The trellis is in two parts and the other half isn't broken at all. I pull myself across the dividing center bar to the other side of the trellis. Take a step down. And another.

"Gus!" Fiona's in the yard below me. Hands cupped around her mouth. "Hang on! Your dad and Coop are getting a ladder."

Hearing that makes my heart kick my ribs. Or, at least, that's what I think at first. It's actually the trellis ripping loose from the side of the house.

Arms flapping, legs kicking, I drop.

Smash into a big, fat bush.

Tumble out.

SMACK! I land on my belly and get a mouthful of grass. Yuck! I spit it out. Roll over. The world spins and I lie still. Close my eyes and wait for my breath to catch up to the rest of me.

Warm fingers brush my cheek. "Gus, are you dead?"

When I open my eyes, Fiona tugs me upright. "Please be all right. You are, aren't you?"

I bob my head. Gingerly poke a sore spot above my right eye.

"Gus?"

At the sound of my dad's voice, I shoot Fiona a look. Puff out. "Got to go. Pinder ranch. Cub."

She flashes me a smile that sends a sizzle all the way to my toes. "Right." She tugs me to my feet. "Come on. I know a short-cut."

TWENTY-SEVEN

It's steamy hot. Bugs dive-bomb through the thickening shadows. I swat them away. Keep going fast to stick with Fiona. When we duck under a low branch, something black as night swoops down. I swear it brushes my head. I swallow my almost shriek. Keep up with Fiona.

This might be a short-cut but the day's shrinking even faster. By the time we reach the beach the fireball sun has sunk. There's only a rosy glow left coating the mirror-flat ocean. Even the sudsy edges of the waves rolling up onto the beach are pink. I'm busy skirting the edges of those waves until Fiona tosses me a challenge. "Race you."

We take off. Arms pumping. Feet pounding the hard-packed sand between the surf's edge and the fenced-off turtle nests. All at once, I'm in the lead. And feeling good about it.

Then Fiona slams on the brakes. Waves to me. "This way."

I gulp a lungful of the salty air on my way back into the jungle. "Wait," I tell her. "My shoes are full of sand."

Fiona comes back to where I flopped down on the warm, sandy ground. Waits with her hands on her knees, while I dump out one tennis shoe at a time. By the time, we're moving again The Preserve has soaked up the last bit of the sunset glow. All the spaces between the trees are deep, dark shadows.

I try to watch where I'm walking. Worry, maybe, I'll step on a snake. Or something. Up ahead, Fiona prances along like she can see just fine. So I stretch out my stride. Pick up the pace.

WHOMP! I stub my toe on something. Go down hard. Land on my hands and knees. "Owwww!"

"Shhh!"

I scramble up. "What?"

Fiona presses a finger against my lips this time. Mouths, *Pinders*.

A shiver ripples through me, which could be from her touching me. Or from the fact that we're really close to the Pinder ranch. In fact, straight ahead, between palm fronds and pine boughs, I catch a glimpse of a house with glowing windows. Once we're even closer I recognize the house, barn and cluster of small sheds from being here with Aunt Willie the day we came to rescue Caspar. Only, tonight, there's no sheriff's car parked by the pickups. And no people anywhere in sight. On the other hand, every first floor window in the house is glowing. So the Pinders must be home. I slip alongside Fiona to ask where she thinks they'd put the cub at the exact second she turns toward me. Our noses bump. I jerk backwards. Would have flopped right on over, if she hadn't grabbed my arm and steadied me.

Her forehead wrinkles as she whispers, "Did you trip *again*?"

I shake my head. Didn't she notice we almost kissed? I straighten up. Yank free. Stand on my own two feet. Point to the barn. And I lead the way to show her who's in charge of this rescue. Only Fiona zips up alongside me. Grabs my arm and tugs me down. We fold up together behind a fan palm as a woman comes out the side door of the house.

Fiona and I exchange *that was close* looks. The woman crosses the dark porch. Wades through the bright puddles of light beneath the line of post lights dotting the yard. When she's closest to us, I see she looks old enough to be a mother. I guess she must be Dirk's mother. I also see she's carrying a metal mixing bowl, which seems a little odd. Unless, maybe, she's taking food to some animal. Like a pet dog.

Or the panther cub.

I look at Fiona. Waggle my eyebrows. She smiles. So she must be thinking the same thing I am.

This is the clue we needed to find the cub. I focus on watching the woman to see where she's going. And planning what to do once she gets there. I'm still hatching a plan when Fiona stands up. Walks straight into the open. And across the same spotlighted part of the yard the woman just crossed.

Geez-mareez!

There's nothing to do but chase after Fiona. Follow her to the ink-dark shadows edging the Pinders' barn. Ahead, around the corner where I can't see, a door creaks open. Thumps shut.

Side by side, Fiona and I flatten against the barn wall. In fact, I press so hard the peeling paint on the wood prickles the backs of my bare arms. But that's not all that's sticking me. I hear Daniel's voice in my head again. *Get out there, Gus. Go. Be the hero.*

So when Fiona starts inching toward the corner of the barn, I snag her arm. Stop sign with my hand.

Fiona's eyes pop open big but she stays. Lets me pass her. I inch along the barn wall alone. At the corner, I lean out.

Slowly.

Just far enough for a peek.

There's a slope-roofed shed against the back of the barn. It doesn't have any windows but the shed door's open a crack. I figure the woman went in there. So I slide around the corner and dash to that door. It's not open enough for me to see inside the shed. So I inch a little closer.

Listen.

There's a swish-swoosh sound like someone walking across gravel. And a scraping noise like metal against metal. Then a chirp.

Oh yeah!

That's the cub.

I practically jump out of my shoes when a woman's voice slices through the nighttime quiet. "Go on now. Eat. It's those meat scraps or nothing. Up to you. I've done my bit by feeding you."

Panic slams me when I hear her start walking again. And the sound keeps getting louder because she must be coming closer to the door.

I dash back to the corner of the barn and around it. Press into the shadows. Pray I got there before she opened the door and saw me. I glance at Fiona who is as stiff-backed against the barn wall as I am. And I hold my breath listening to the shed door shut.

A second later, the woman marches right past me. And Fiona.

Luckily, she never once glances our way.

Finally, the woman is crossing the yard on her way back to the house. I watch. Wait. And the second she goes inside the house, I launch. Run back to the shed door. Fiona's right behind me when I open it and slip inside.

There's no light on in the shed but the back wall is the barn wall. Light is streaming through cracks in that, striping everything around us. Saddles. Bridles. Harnesses. Horse blankets. And the panther cub inside its cage.

Seeing us the cub stops pawing at the wall of the cage. Chirps.

Fiona and I rush to it. She croons, "Poor baby. Now that we know it's here, we've got to go tell Willie. Have her call the sheriff."

I shake my head. "We've got to get the cub out of here."

Fiona asks the question I'm thinking. "How?"

TWENTY-EIGHT

I look at the panther cub watching me through the walls of its cage. "I'm going to have to carry it."

Fiona's eyes go big. "You're going to carry that cage all the way to Wahkullah House?"

"Nope." I lean down. "Gonna carry the cub."

"Oh. Be careful." Her face scrunches up. "It could bite and scratch."

"I'll be careful." The cub backs up as far as it can inside the cage. I'm kind of glad it's a little scared. Because I'm scared too. A whole lot more scared than I want Fiona to know.

"I'm not going to hurt you," I say. "I'm going to get you out of here. Away from the nasty ole Pinders. So don't bite me. Okay?"

The cub crouches down. Its ears lie flat.

I reach into the cage.

Fiona leans down too. Wiggles her fingers. "Here kitty."

The panther cub explodes out of the cage. Shoots past me too fast to grab. Lands kicking up gravel and takes off running.

I spring. Chase after it.

The cub scoots for a hole in the barn wall. Scrambles half way through it. I do the football tackle Daniel taught me. Wrap my arms around the cub. Pull it back. It hisses. Swipes with claws out as I—somehow—stand up with it in my arms.

Yeow! That's me being scratched.

YEOWL! That's the cub attacking with teeth and claws as it wiggles. Fights to be free.

"Hang on!" Fiona calls. She's grabbed a saddle blanket off a peg on the wall. She throws the blanket over the cub.

Together we wrap up the cub's legs and body so only its head pokes out. It spits and struggles but I still hold on. Tight.

Fiona flips back her ponytail and grins. "I don't believe you did that."

"We did that." I feel my cheeks pump up as I smile too.

Then there's the sound of the barn door sliding open.

Fiona presses both hands over her mouth.

The bright stripes streaking from the barn into the shed go dark for an instant. Someone is walking around inside the barn. The cub yowls again and fear washes over me.

Bang! Thump! Something smacks the barn wall. "Grab that end. Come on."

I'm sure that voice is Dirk's dad.

Fiona's eyes pop. I'm so scared I'm weak-kneed and sick to my stomach. But I stay on my feet. Swallow the bitter taste in my mouth. And I keep my grip on the cub. It's easier now, though, because it's stopped struggling. When I look down, the cub is looking up at me.

I have to be brave. For this little guy. And Fiona.

I nod toward the door. We sneak to it. Fiona eases the door open just far enough. We slip out of the shed. Into the dark night. Hustle along the side of the barn. Across the yard, through the puddles of light, to the house.

I look around. No one is following us. Fiona taps my arm, points to a parked pickup truck, and holds her hand to her ear like she has a phone. Mouths *Call Coop*.

I shake my head. There's no way to know there's a cell phone in the truck.

She hustles over to the pickup anyway. So I follow to stick with her.

"But, Dad. Why do I have to go along?" Dirk the Jerk's voice is coming from the direction of the barn. He must have been in there with his father.

George Pinder answers, "Because I need your help."

Scared to my bones, I look around for an escape route. Don't see any way to run to The Preserve that isn't in the open. In full view of the Pinders. And I'm holding the cub they kidnapped. Well, I guess that's technically catnapped.

George Pinder says, "Go on, Dirk. Get in the truck."

Fiona's on the driver's side of the pickup with the door open. Leaning in searching. I'm on the passenger's side. We exchange *O.M.G. looks* through the cab's window.

I mouth *Down!*

She backs up. Eases the door shut. Vanishes. I hear her scramble under the pickup. I crouch down too, hugging tight to the wrapped up cub.

"Hey, kid, come here and help me carry this box."

I recognize Marcus Pinder's voice. Puff in relief when gravel crunching lets me know Dirk's heading back to the barn to help his uncle.

Then I hear a hiss but it's not the cub. It's behind me. I look over my shoulder and see Fiona peeking around the end of the truck's bed. Her face wears a silver mask in the moonlight. The rest of her is hidden in shadow but I see her fingers signal *follow me.*

TWENTY-NINE

My legs pump. My feet pound the ground. My back's sweat-pasted to my shirt. And my arms burn from running with the cub. I shift the heavy-as-a-big-sack-of-flour bundle to rest on one hip. That helps till the cat kicks me. Stretches out of the towel enough to rub a furry cheek and a wet nose against my neck.

"Wait."

Fiona trots back to where I'm struggling with my furry passenger. "Hey cub, calm down. Gus is saving you."

We work together to tuck the towel back around the cub.

At last, I'm hugging it against my chest again. The baby panther stares at me with big blue eyes. "You don't want the Pinders to get you back. Believe me. So stay still. Let me carry you."

"What do you think the Pinders were moving in the dark?"

"Don't know. But probably nothing good. Okay, let's go."

Fiona pats my shoulder. "It's not much farther."

We walk instead of run now. Maybe that's why it still feels a long ways pushing through brush that slaps back at me. Snags my shorts and shirt and my bare arms.

At last, we break out of the brush and wade through a field of thigh-high ferns all silver-washed by moonlight. Straight ahead on the far side I see the tree tunnel I know leads to Wahkullah House.

I give the cub a little squeeze. "Almost home."

Hey! That's funny. I actually feel like I'm headed home. How did that happen?

Fiona bounds ahead but stops short of the towering live oaks and waits for me. She's standing in a puddle of moonlight and even in that silvery light her hair is amazingly—cross my heart—the color of honey.

I smile.

She smiles back at me. "Cub still doing okay?"

It divides a look between us and mews.

"Guess that means *yes*."

"I think that means *thank you*." Fiona flips her ponytail over her shoulder. "You rescued it."

"It was a team effort." We march down the tunnel of trees, side-by-side. Fiona takes long steps, matching her strides to mine.

"Well, I would never—ever—have chased the cub, like you did. Or caught it. But who knows what the Pinders planned to do with it. Sure, they might have traded it for the whale's tooth map but they might have done something else." Fiona's face goes all pinches and puckers. "Something bad."

I nod. "I know."

"Well." Fiona smiles. "That makes you the cub's hero."

I don't say anything. I do replay that last bit in my head a few times, though, while I walk alongside Fiona. Through the tree tunnel. Toward Wahkullah House with its windows glowing a welcome.

Then twin beams of light slice through the dark from behind us. And an engine's revving is a monster's roar. I swing around. See the Pinders' pickup truck racing toward us. Fiona leaps one way. I charge the other. The cub shrieks. Fights me. It's too fierce to hold now. The baby panther explodes from my arms. Leaps to the ground. Runs into the dark.

Brakes screech. Tires crunch. Dirt billows and swallows us all. A truck door swings open.

"You're not besting me this time." George Pinder charges straight at me.

I take off and run flat out until I realize George Pinder isn't chasing me. Or Fiona. When I stop and turn around, I see he has the cub by the scruff of the neck. He hauls it to the front of the pickup. Holds the cat in that spotlight. Through the dust sifting down from the dark George Pinder looks me straight in the eye. "See what I've got, kid? I'm gonna wring its neck unless—"

"You wouldn't!" I holler. "It's just a baby."

He shakes his head. "Get me the whale's tooth—the real one this time—or say bye-bye, baby."

Dirk leans out the pickup's window. "Better do it, Gus."

And, right then, the panther cub screams.

I put my head down and charge. Ram George Pinder in the belly. Kick. Punch. He shoves me down but I scramble right back up. Charge into him.

This time, I take a punch to the cheek that hurts like a whole nest of wasp stings. And the next punch comes quick from the other direction. Clips my ear and makes my head ring. When I duck that punch, it dawns on me. George Pinder's swinging with both fists.

The cub's loose!

Somebody blasts the truck's horn a couple of times. I duck as Pinder's arm swoops over my head. And I give his belly my best jab. Then I dart out of the way. Stay clear of his next punch.

Now there's headlights streaking our way from Wahkullah House. And Fiona's whooping and jumping up and down. Waving stretched-high arms.

George Pinder's long legs pump. He kicks up dust on his way to the pickup. Hauls open the truck's door and scoots into the driver's seat.

Raindrops pelt me. And, for just an instant, everything goes dazzling bright, when lightning rips open the nighttime sky. But I don't run from the rain this time. That's because I see the cub in the grass at the foot of one of the tall live oaks.

"There," I whisper and turn to Fiona. I know she's seen the cub too when our eyes meet. I feel the smile she gives me all the way to my bones. And she quickly heads down the tunneled road, waving for who's coming to stop.

I hold out my hand to the cub. "C'mon, little one. We're home. Let me help you."

And, step-by-step,
slowly,
I slip
closer.

THIRTY

Rain pounds on the house roof like a million tacks. The power's off, but yet another lightning flash lights up Aunt Willie's dark kitchen. Spotlights Coop spooning ice cream into root beer floats. Dad's lighting a tray full of fat, white candles. Aunt Willie's perched on a tall stool with the wall phone's receiver to her ear and the dangling long cord casting wiggling snake shadows on the wall.

I suppose the lightning spotlights me too because the panther cub in the travel cage by the sofa is staring at me with glowing eyes. So I bite my lip and act brave while Fiona dabs stinging stuff on my cheek.

"Almost done. There. Now, I'll get your drink." Fiona's ponytail swishes as she walks away.

I sink to the floor by the travel cage and lean over to look at the cub. When its eyes meet mine, I tell him. "Don't worry about the rain. You're safe here. This is home. Well, until you're big and strong enough to live wild and free."

Fiona prances up carrying her root beer float and delivering mine. She sits down beside me. "So you saved the panther cub twice. I think that's earned you naming rights. What's its name going to be?"

I'm thinking when Aunt Willie hooks the phone in its cradle. Turns to take us all in with a sweeping look. "Okay. I've got the scoop."

"You've got two scoops." Coop hands her a foam-topped glass and his grin flashes gold in the candlelight.

"Very funny." Aunt Willie smiles. "I'm talking about the Pinders."

"Which is why I made us root beer floats." Coop flops down on the sofa behind me. "Spill."

"Okay. I have it on good authority. George and Marcus Pinder have been arrested. Yes, assault on a minor tops the list. However, the charges don't stop there, although we can't actually prove they took an endangered Florida panther cub."

Our combined booing interrupts until Aunt Willie waves us to silence.

"No. Wait. What they were moving tonight was loggerhead turtle eggs. The U.S. Fish and Wildlife Service has been watching them. They set up an undercover operation to catch them selling the turtle eggs to what they thought was a restaurant owner. Turns out there's a law, The Lacey Act, against doing that. They'll be fined. They could go to jail."

"Ahhh," Coop sighs. "Don't think even a Pinder judge can keep that family out of all the trouble they're in this time."

Right then—no kidding—the grandfather clock in the hall

upstairs bongs a whole bunch of times.

Aunt Willie checks her watch. "Well, my goodness, and the time's right. How about that."

Fiona beams. Lifts both hands like she's signaling victory. "The Wahkullah House Spirit is pleased."

"I know I am." Dad crosses to the sofa in long strides and sits beside Coop.

Fiona rocks up on her knees. "And we've still got the real whale's tooth map so we can keep working on where Gasparilla's gold is buried."

Coop stabs the air. "Wish I could prove the Pinders were the ones wrecked my house. Make them pay for the damage."

Aunt Willie licks her straw and points it at Coop. "Technically it's George Pinder's house."

"But it was my mess." Coop stands up. "Guess I need a second root beer float to feel better. Anybody else want one?"

The cub chirps.

I point at the panther. "Gasparilla said *yes*."

Coop's frown tucks into his scar. "Gasparilla? You're naming the cub after a pirate?"

Everyone chimes in with an opinion about that.

"Hey." Nobody hears me over the rumbling boom of thunder. I stand up as the night quiets down. Everyone stops talking and each shadow-streaked face gives me a *what's up* look. I spread my arms wide. "I say Gasparilla's the right name because that panther cub's going to have golden eyes when it grows up. And—well—I treasure it."

"Oh." Aunt Willie presses fingers to her lips.

"Okay," Coop booms. "You convinced me."

Fiona leans around me to wave at the cub. "Hello, Gasparilla."

Then the phone rings.

"Really?" Aunt Willie's face scrunches. "I hate talking on the phone during storms."

Coop reaches over her shoulder and grabs the phone. "I'll take a message. It could be important."

"More likely somebody selling flood insurance. Hello?" She trades her drink glass for the phone and Coop plods on to the refrigerator.

I sit back down to finish my float but mostly I watch Aunt Willie and wonder what's up. Her toes tap. Her knees jiggle. And, like twin rockets launching, her eyebrows arch so high they disappear under her frizzy bangs. When she hangs up, she squeals long and shrill.

Dad leaps up. "What's wrong?"

Aunt Willie flaps her arms. "Nothing's wrong. In fact, it's very right. That was Janet James."

"Oh, she's so sweet." Fiona shapes her fingers to display a heart. "Her dog Ralphie loves my cookies."

Aunt Willie clamps her hands over her knees. "So she said. She also said her nephew, the deputy sheriff, called to tell her what happened. And how we rescued the panther cub again. She wants—and I quote—to do her part for the wildlife shelter."

Coop stops licking the ice cream scoop. "Meaning?"

"She's setting up a foundation to support it." Aunt Willie's smile is toothy bright in the candlelight. "We're supposed to come up with an official name for the shelter and she'll set up an account at the bank."

"Like to deposit money?" Dad asks.

Aunt Willie nods. "Turns out Janet James is a whole lot wealthier than anyone knew. She's promised the shelter one million dollars. Each year. For five years."

Coop's whoop is thunderous.

Fiona leaps up. "I'll bake Ralphie cookies forever."

"Wait. The best part is Janet James wants the foundation to focus on protecting Florida panthers." Aunt Willie flaps her hands. "I can study them. And these big cats can have a future on Pine Island."

Dad steps around me. Hugs Aunt Willie. Fiona hooks arms with Coop and they dance.

I sink back against the sofa. My frown digs in all the way to my cheekbones. Tears pile up, blur everything and spill.

Fiona's toe-nudge on my leg makes me jerk up straight. She shoots me a *what's wrong* look. I can't say it out loud but the words shout in my head.

There's no future for Daniel! He didn't have time to do anything people will remember.

Aunt Willie points at Coop. "Listen. You need a new place to live and I need help. I'll give you any cabin you want to fix up for yourself at Wahkullah House, if you'll just, please, help me run the shelter."

My throat's so tight I have to shove the words out. "The Daniel Hart Wildlife Shelter."

Fiona crosses her hands over her heart. "That's the perfect name for the shelter."

Aunt Willie nods. "Abso-total-lutely."

Coop's good eye winks at me. "It'll be my pleasure to make the Daniel Hart Wildlife Shelter world class."

Fiona plants her hands on her hips. "Well, you won't do it without my help."

"Definitely going to be a lot of work, I'm guessing." Dad says. "Gus, I rescheduled our flight for tomorrow but, maybe, we should talk about you staying here for the rest of the summer. What do you think?"

"I think GREAT!" I feel my grin stretch ear to ear as the happiness soaks in.

THIRTY-ONE

It's after midnight. I know because the grandfather clock outside my bedroom door just finished bonging. I plump my pillow. Roll over. Shut my eyes but can't shut down my brain. I'm happy I'm staying to help with the shelter this summer and I'm kind of glad we haven't found the pirate treasure—*yet*. But that's started me thinking about the future beyond this summer. Wondering about it a little.

When wind gusts flap the curtains, I dash to the window seat. Reach across and shut the window just as thunder booms. And in his cage by my feet Gasparilla mews and whines. The storm never let up enough to take the panther cub out to the cabins. So before he went to bed in the guestroom down the hall, Coop carried the cat in its cage up to my room for the night. I figured the cub must be scared and I convinced Coop it shouldn't be alone.

"It's okay, Gasparilla," I tell him. "I'll take care of you."

I sit down cross-legged on the floor watching the panther cub fussing, and bit by bit, a song comes to me. Fills my head until I think I'll burst if I don't let it out.

I twist around to reach under the bed for the leather case I stuffed there. Flick the latches up. Lift out the guitar Coop gave me for someday when I want to play again.

I think that's now. Then I think maybe it's not.

I sit there with the guitar cradled in my arms. Listen some more to the thunder and the rain. The song in my brain floods in along with memories of the flash flood. How Daniel came back for me. Saved me.

That song in my head won't quit. I pluck the guitar strings. When the panther cub goes quiet. I play some more. Notes become chords. Next a melody.

The second time through a riff slips in. Third time, words whisper to me. Gasparilla settles down when I sing to him. Sing what I hear in my head.

A creak makes me stop and look up. Dad's standing in the doorway. "You write that song?"

I nod.

He crosses to me in long strides.

I stand up and lay the guitar on the bed. Dad cups my cheek with his warm hand. My chin's quivering but I push the words out. "I always want to remember Daniel. Even if it hurts."

"Me too." Dad's chin and words jiggle just like mine. "I'm never going to forget how much I owe your brother for saving you."

"Me either." I hug him. "I love you, Dad."

Right then the panther cub chirps really loud. I drop to my knees to check if it's okay. I look straight into Gasparilla's eyes. Maybe it's my welling-up tears, but, cross my heart, I swear that panther's eyes are already starting to look golden.

READER'S CLUB

Discover More

About Florida Panthers

Florida panthers are among the most rare big cats in the world. They only live in Florida's swampy forests, and scientists believe only around a hundred remain. These big cats live solo, pairing up only to mate. And cubs usually only stay with their mother for about two years. Although alligators may kill these cats, people are a much bigger threat. While laws make it illegal, some people still kill them—sometimes out of concern for pets and livestock. People cause even more problems for panthers by cutting down forests and building on the land.

Key to helping Florida panthers is to preserve their forest habitat. What makes that difficult is that so many people are moving to Florida. And each panther needs a large home range to roam over while hunting. Males may range over 200 square miles (517 square km); females about 80 square miles (207 square km). But those ranges need to connect so pairs can mate and produce cubs. Besides setting aside areas of natural habitat for them, programs are underway to breed Florida panthers in captivity and then release these cats into suitable wild areas.

• Florida panthers can run as fast as 35 miles per hour (56 kph), but only in short bursts. They usually sneak close to their prey and pounce.

• Males can be as long as 7 feet (2.1 m) from nose to tail tip. They can weigh as much as 160 pounds (about 72 kg). Females are somewhat smaller.

• Florida panthers are carnivores, hunting and eating prey animals. They mainly hunt deer and wild pigs but also hares and mice.

• Mothers only produce a litter of one to three cubs every two years. Cubs only develop for about three months before birth. Their eyes open after two to three weeks and are blue for four to six months, when they turn gold. Their coat is also spotted at first and the spots fade as they mature.

• Footprint - About 3 inches (7.6 cm) wide by 3 inches (7.6 cm) long. Front feet are slightly wider than back feet. Key to identifying their footprint is the 3-lobed pad print (not really a heel because these cats walk on their toes). As they walk, their hind feet are often placed in the print of their front feet. An adult's track is about the size of a standard baseball.

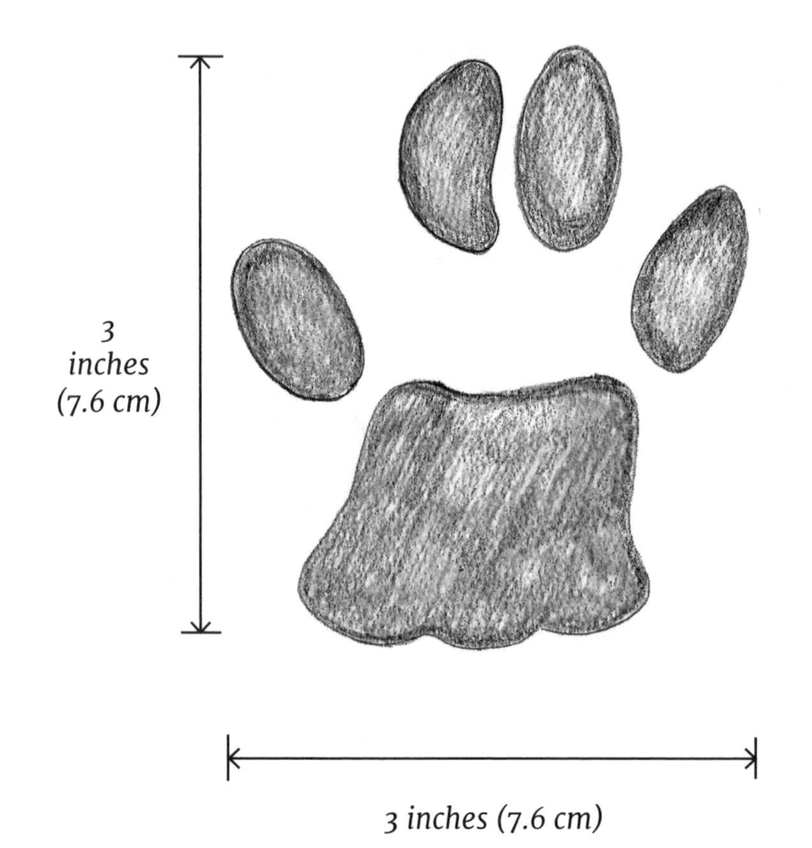

Florida Panther

About Loggerhead Turtles

While scientists don't know the total number of loggerhead turtles in the ocean, they believe there are around 50,000 nesting females. The population appears to be decreasing, and loggerheads are now listed as "threatened". Adults are at risk of being caught in fishing nets and drowning. They may also swallow plastic trash floating in the ocean and die. Young turtles are prey for many ocean animals. The turtle eggs are eaten by crabs, foxes, and raccoons. Though there are laws to protect them, people sometimes also catch turtles or dig up the eggs to eat.

Key to helping loggerhead turtles is protecting their nesting sites. The main nesting location is Masirah Island in the Arabian Sea. Each year, as many as 30,000 females come ashore to nest there. The second most important loggerhead turtle nesting site is the southeastern United States, mainly Florida. About 15,000 females lay eggs there annually. It's important to keep known nesting beaches clean. Then during the nesting season (April through September) "DO NOT DISTURB"!

- Loggerheads get their name from their extra big head.
- An adult loggerhead is likely to weigh as much as 300 pounds (136 kg) and have a shell a little over 3 feet (1 m) long.
- Loggerhead turtles are omnivores, meaning they eat both plants and animals.
- Turtles may live to be 60 years old. Female loggerheads usually don't start nesting until they are between 10 and 30 years old. Then they only nest and lay eggs every two to three years.
- Only one in 1,000 hatchlings survives to become an adult.
- Footprint - When a female loggerhead turtle crawls ashore to lay her eggs, marks are left by her front flippers. Track shows alternating leg movement. The trail is about 25 inches (63.5 cm) wide.

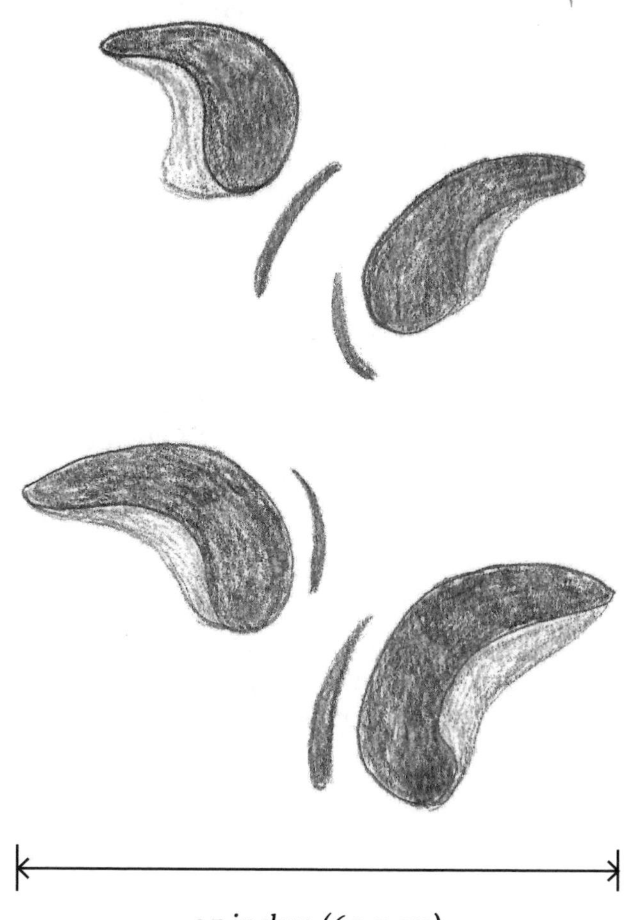

25 inches (63.5 cm)

Loggerhead Turtle

More Wildlife Fast Facts

American Alligator

• Alligators have 74 to 80 teeth in their big jaws. New teeth move in to replace any that are lost.

• Alligators continue to grow throughout their lifetime. Males are slightly longer than females.

• A female lays 20 to 50 eggs and buries them with sand, mud, and plant matter. Then she guards the nest from hungry predators. The temperature at the nest site determines if the babies that hatch will be males or females. Cooler temperatures between 82 and 86 degrees F (27 to 30 C) produce females. Warmer temperatures between 90 and 93 degrees F (32 to 33 C) produce males. Moderate in-between temperatures produce a mix of males and females.

• Footprint - Only three toes on each foot have claws. Back feet have 4 toes. Front feet have 5 toes. The bigger the gator the bigger its footprint. Florida has recorded a male a little over 14 feet (4.2 m) long and weighing about 1,000 pounds (453.59 kg). An average 6 foot long alligator has the following footprint: Front foot about 8 inches (20.32 cm) wide by 10 inches (25.4 cm) long; Back foot is about 10 inches (25.4 cm) wide by 12 inches (30.48 cm) long. Back footprint shows partial webbing between center toes. Footprints may be wiped out by body and tail drag.

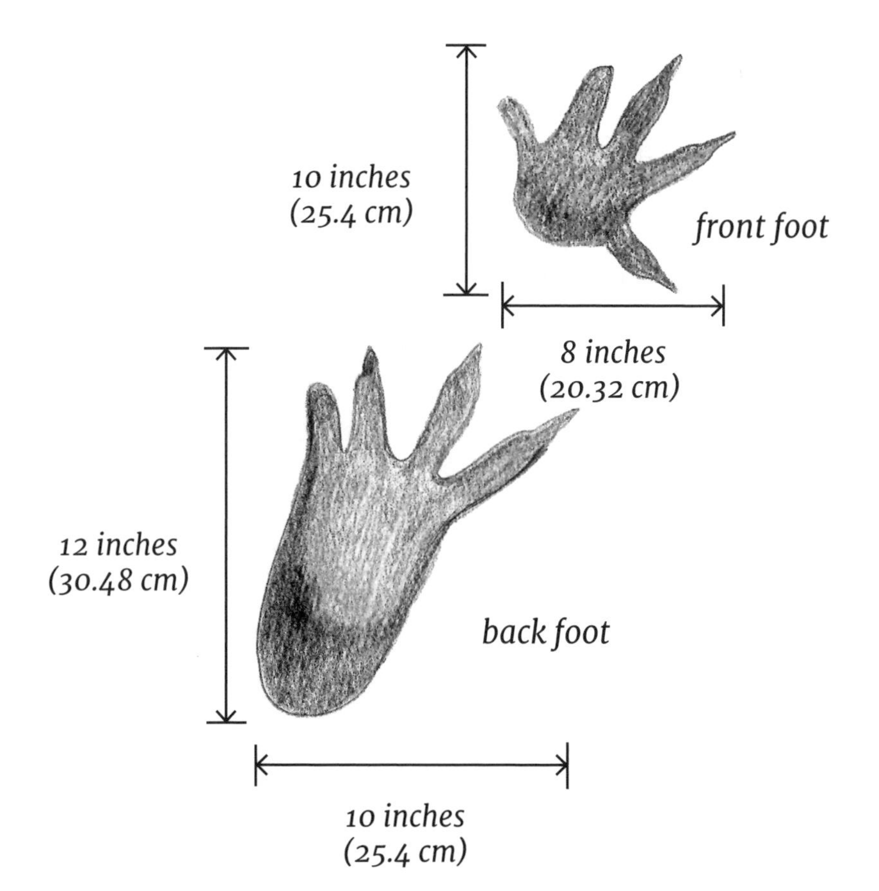
10 inches
(25.4 cm)
front foot
8 inches
(20.32 cm)
12 inches
(30.48 cm)
back foot
10 inches
(25.4 cm)

Alligator

Florida Bonneted Bat

• Each mother bat gives birth to just one baby per breeding season. However, females may have two breeding seasons per year.

• Florida bonneted bats mainly eat flying insects. They use echolocation (blasting out sounds and listening for echoes) to detect insects as much as 15 feet (4.5 m) away.

• These bats have a wingspan that spreads up to 20 inches (50.8 cm).

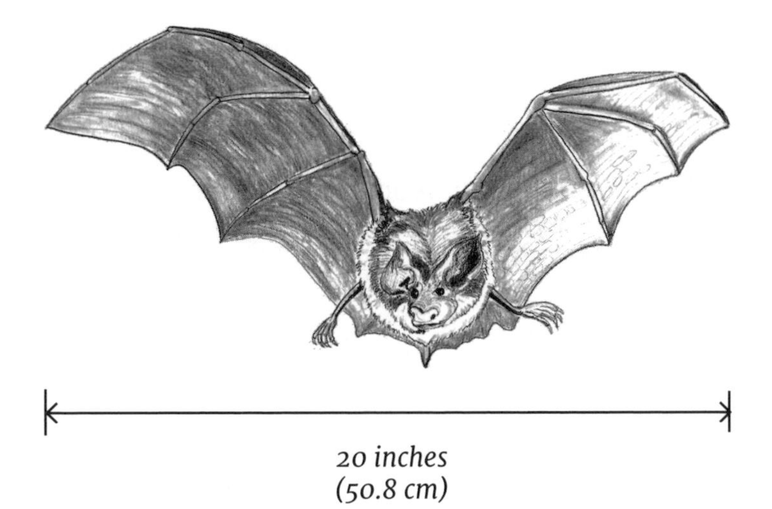

20 inches
(50.8 cm)

Florida Bonneted Bat

Brown Pelican

• Brown pelicans dive into water to catch fish. Upon surfacing, they tip their bills downward to drain out water before swallowing.

• This bird incubates its eggs by covering them with its webbed feet.

• Pelican pouches can hold 3 gallons (11.3 liters) of water.

• Track shows toes and webbing in between all toes. Feet are 7 inches (17.78 cm) long and 4 ½ inches (11.43 cm) wide.

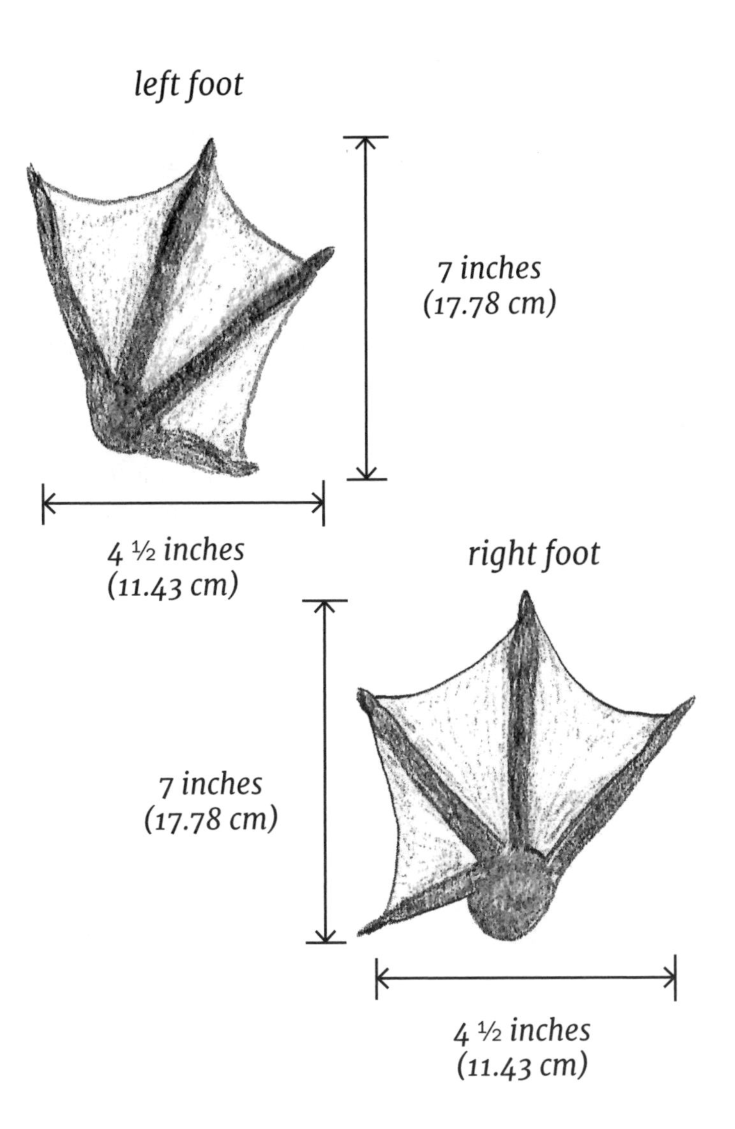

Brown Pelican

Coyote

• Coyotes have been recorded running as fast as 40 miles per hour (64kph). They can also jump as far as 13 feet (4 m).

• They make lots of different sounds: howls, yelps, barks, growls, wails, and squeals. Making sounds lets them express themselves and keep track of family members.

• Coyotes have such keen hearing that in the winter they can locate prey hiding in tunnels under the snow. Then pounce to catch a meal.

• Front feet are slightly bigger than back feet. Front foot 2½ inches (6.35 cm) wide by 2 inches (5 cm) long. Back foot 2¼ inches (5.7 cm) wide by 1¾ inches (4.4 cm) long. Toenails may leave marks.

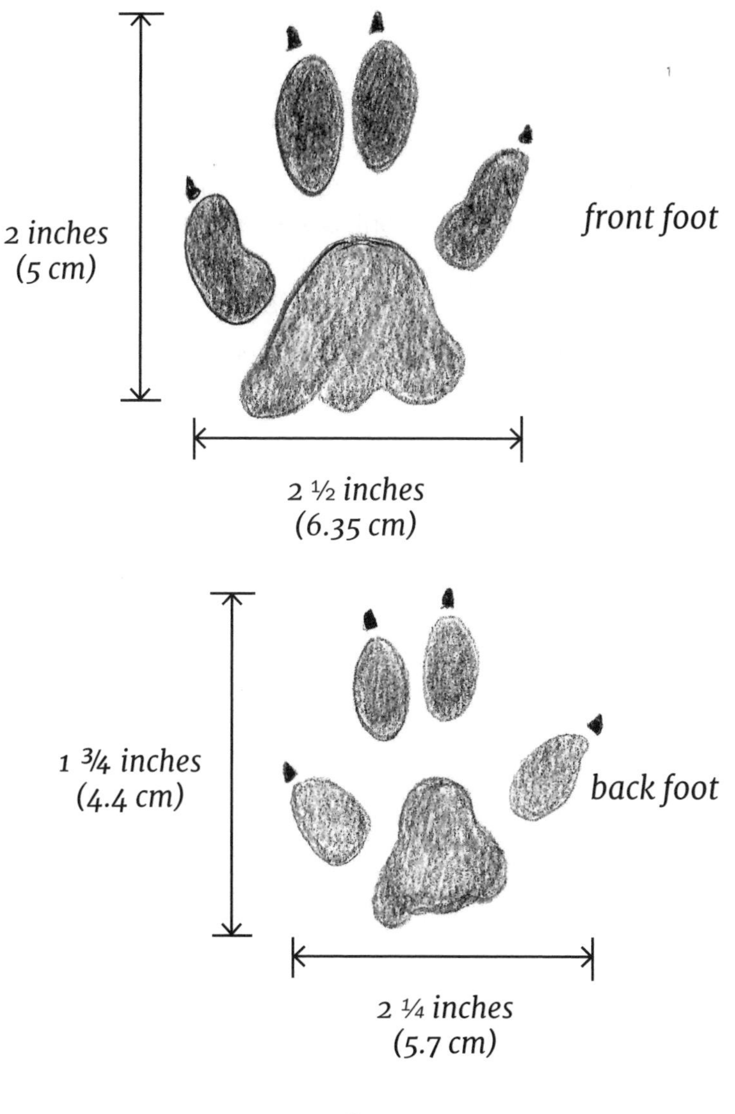
2 inches
(5 cm)
front foot
2 ½ inches
(6.35 cm)
1 ¾ inches
(4.4 cm)
back foot
2 ¼ inches
(5.7 cm)

Coyote

Striped Skunk

• Skunks can direct their stream of smelly liquid to strike a target up to 10 feet (3 m) away.

• When they feel threatened, skunks stamp their feet and lift their tail as a warning. They only spray as a last resort. They can spray several times. Then it may take as long as ten days for them to build up enough liquid to spray again.

• Skunks will eat nearly anything they can find: plants, insects, worms, eggs, reptiles and fish.

• Front foot is a little over an inch wide (3 cm) and 1 ¾ inches (4.4 cm) long. Back foot is about 1 ¼ inches (3.1 cm) wide and 2 inches (5 cm) long.

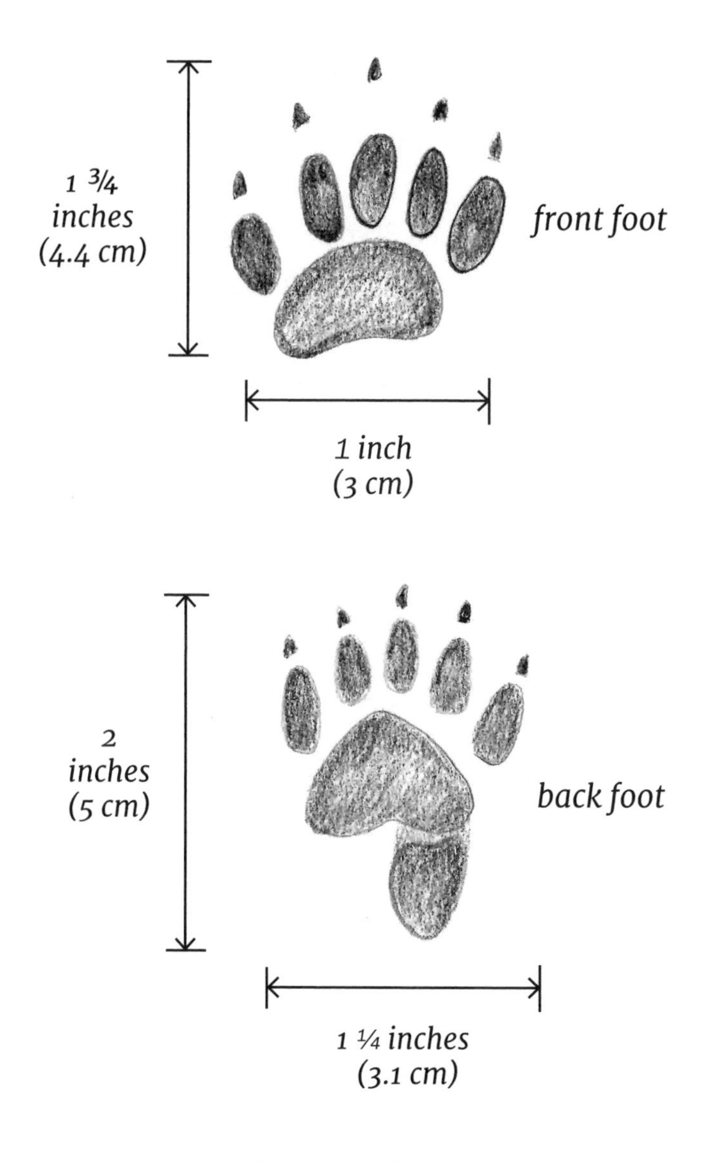

Striped Skunk

White-Tailed Deer

• Only male deer grow antlers. These are shed and regrown each year.

• Deer can run as fast as 30 miles per hour (48 kph).

• They can leap as high as 10 feet (3 m) and jump as far as 30 feet (9 m) in a single bound.

• When running from danger, deer lift their tail, like a flag, alerting other deer that are nearby.

• A deer's foot is two elongated toes, each capped in a hard toenail, called a hoof. The bigger the deer the bigger its track but usually an adult male (called a buck) makes a print about 3 inches (7.62 cm) long. For better traction, toes spread apart differently depending on the ground.

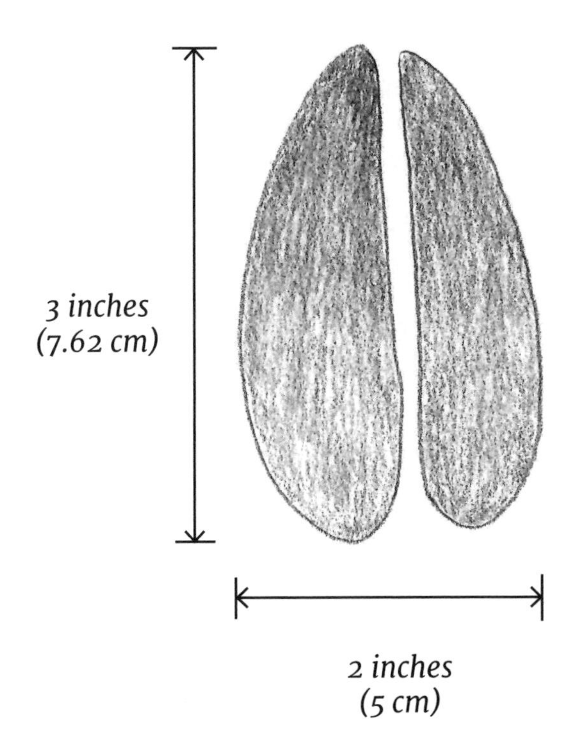

White-Tailed Deer

Wild Boar

• Wild boar use their rubbery snouts to dig for roots and bulbs to eat.

• In winter, they have a double coat: thick, bristly hairs on top of a soft undercoat.

• Their upper and lower canine teeth are tusks (teeth so long they stick out of their mouths). Lower tusks grow longest, as long as 4 $^{5}/_{7}$ inches (12 cm). Males have longer tusks than females. Tusks are mainly for defense. Males also use them to fight for mates.

• Footprint - There are two toes and they leave prints about 2 ¾ inch (7 cm) wide and 4 inches (10.16 cm) long. Wild boar have a more rounded footprint than white-tailed deer tracks.

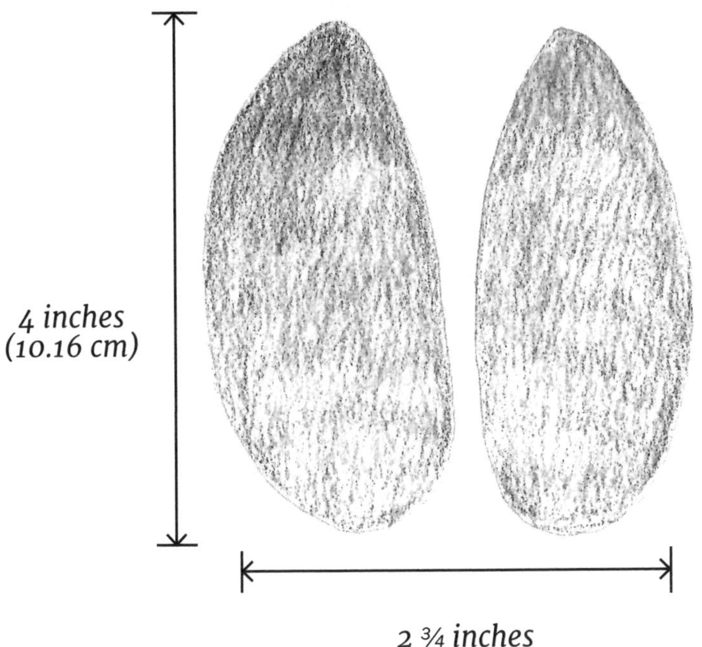

Wild Boar

Raccoon

- They're active at night.

- Use their front paws and finger-like toes to grab food fast. They catch and eat crayfish, frogs, mice and dig up turtle eggs.

- Babies develop for only about 63 days before being born. Mother raccoon gives birth to just one to as many as seven babies. She raises them on her own.

- They're good swimmers and tree climbers.

- Footprint - Front foot is almost 2 ⅞ inches (7.3 cm) wide and 3 ⅛ inches (7.9 cm) long. The hind foot is about 3 inches (7.6 cm) wide and 4 inches (10 cm) long. A raccoon walks flat-footed.

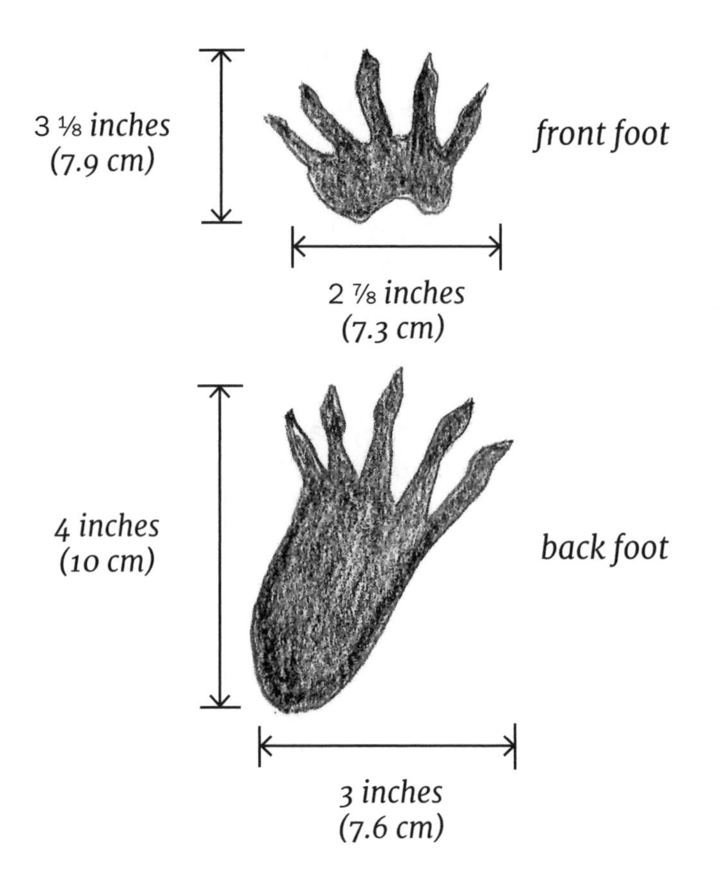
3 ⅛ inches
(7.9 cm)
front foot
2 ⅞ inches
(7.3 cm)
4 inches
(10 cm)
back foot
3 inches
(7.6 cm)

Raccoon

Action Pack

Things To Think About

1. How does Gus feel about Coop at the beginning of the story? How do his feelings toward him change, and why?

2. Gus was so afraid of rainstorms at the beginning of the story he would run for shelter at the first drops. But after the cub runs away from George Pinder, Gus stays outside even though it's raining. Why does he push past his fear?

3. Coop whips up root beer floats anytime anyone is upset and needs to feel better. What do you do when you are feeling sad or overwhelmed, or when you just want to feel cheered up?

4. Throughout the story, Gus, Fiona, and Coop are on a quest to find Gasparilla's buried treasure. Why do you think, at the end of the story, Gus feels glad they haven't found it—*yet?* Can you think of a time you worked on something you enjoyed so much you didn't want doing it to end?

Things To Do

* Coop is always turning things that are junk into something that's both totally cool and useful. Try to think of at least six different ways you could reuse containers, such as plastic water bottles, egg cartons, or sturdy drink cups. Here are two to get you started.

Play Jug Toss. Rinse clean two galloon-sized milk jugs. Use scissors to cut one side off each milk jug. You may want an adult partner to help with that. Now use a soft foam ball to play. The goal is to use the milk jug scoops to toss the ball from one person to the other. Any player who fails to catch the ball collects one letter of the word "Oops." When all four letters are collected by the same person, the other person wins the game. Multiply the fun by making more scoops and having more players.

Light Up Your Life. Save your balloons when they pop. Stretch the colored rubber over the bulb end of your flashlight and pull it smooth. Have an adult help by anchoring this in place with a rubber band. Then wait until dark (or go into a closet) and switch on the flashlight for a special effect. Try making several different colored flashlights. Explore what happens when the different beams of colored light overlap.

* For Market Day, Fiona bakes cookies shaped like animals at the wildlife shelter. You don't have to bake to make animals with this dough. And the cookies will, abso-total-lutely, be yummy.

Whip Up Animal Cookies. In a bowl, mix together 1 cup of creamy peanut butter and 1 tablespoon of runny honey. Stir in enough dry milk powder to make a stiff dough. With an adult partner, collect a variety of extras that are safe to eat. Some possibilities are raisins, nuts, small carrot sticks, miniature chocolate chips, licorice whips, and shredded coconut. Next, shape animal bodies out of the dough. Use the extras to create your animal cookies.

Fast Facts About Sandra Markle

Sandra has two children: Scott and Holly; and three grandchildren – Allison, Jacob and Piper.

She also has a cat named Beau. He's her current cat but there is always a cat to curl up next to her while she's writing. Or bug her to take a break and play with the cat.

Her entire house is where she writes because she works on a laptop. All she needs is a place to put her feet up—and room for Beau to curl up.

She loves animals of all kinds and writes about lots of different animals. It gives her an excuse to study them—and when possible, spend time in the wild with them. But, if you wonder why Gus is always on the lookout for snakes in this story, ask her about her experience with the boa constrictor.

She also loves to paint and so there are pictures on most walls—many of animals, some of past pet cats.

Sandra lives in Florida but she has lived in Ohio (where she grew up), North Carolina, Texas, Georgia, New Zealand, and Antarctica (yes, even during one winter, BRRRRRRRRR!).